all rivers flow to the sea

all rivers flow to the sea

Alison McGhee

CANDLEWICK PRESS
CAMBRIDGE, MASSACHUSETTS

First edition 2005

Library of Congress Cataloging-in Publication Data
McGhee, Alison
All rivers flow to the sea / Alison McGhee. —1st ed.
p. cm.
Summary: After a car accident in the Adirondacks leaves her older sister Ivy brain-dead, seventeen-year-old Rose struggles with her grief and guilt as she slowly learns to let her sister go.
ISBN 0-7636-2591-4
[1. Sisters—Fiction. 2. Traffic accidents—Fiction. 3. Love—Fiction. 4. Grief—Fiction. 5. Death—Fiction. 6. Adirondack Mountains (N.Y.)—Fiction.] I. Title.
PZ7.M4784675Al 2005
[Fic]—dc22 2004054609

2 4 6 8 10 9 7 5 3 1

Printed in the United States of America

This book was typeset in Granjon.

Candlewick Press
2067 Massachusetts Avenue
Cambridge, Massachusetts 02140

visit us at www.candlewick.com

To Laurel Blackett, Kate DiCamillo, Holly McGhee,
Julie Schumacher, Ellen Harris Swiggett, and Meredith Wade—
sisters all

CHAPTER ONE

Here is the school bus. Here is the school bus door, chuffing open with its familiar wheeze. Here are the school bus steps. Put your right foot on the bottom one. Haul your left leg up to the next. Here is mean Katie the bus driver, scowling out the big bus window. Here is your backpack, heavy and hurting your shoulders. Where is your sister Ivy who should be behind you, shoving at you to hurry up? Ivy is not here. You and your sister had an accident. Now you are on the bus. Walk down the aisle. There's an empty seat. Sit down. Now everyone is on the bus. Now Katie shuts the door and shoves the big black gear stick.

Your first day back is over. The bell that is not a bell has blared, and the school day is over.

Jimmy Wilson is next to you on the old green vinyl seat. Jimmy Wilson, who has been silently in love with you since kindergarten. The bus jolts and bumps and groans and grinds its way around the curves of the Sterns Gorge. You are back on the bus.

Your sister Ivy and you had an accident.

The world should have stopped, but it didn't.

One month has passed since that day of the accident, the accident that you and your sister were in. One month has passed since that day at the end of March when time plucked you up and set you down again, here in this new place. In that month, Katie the bus driver stopped wearing her Dairylea windbreaker and Jimmy Wilson stopped wearing the fur hat that his uncle brought back from Russia. No more winter boots. No more mittens and scarves. Brown grass is now green. Every class has marched on: Goodbye, *Romeo and Juliet;* hello, *Hamlet.* Goodbye, World War II; hello, Korea. Goodbye, rudiments of string theory, and hello, chaos complexity.

Your sister Ivy and you had an accident. The world should have stopped, but it didn't. The world kept on going.

How can the world just keep on going? An earthquake in India kills a thousand people, and the world keeps on going. A famine in China kills a million people, and the world keeps on going. The twin towers of the World Trade Center buckle and fall, and the world, the world keeps on going.

You get up in the morning. You go to the bathroom. You make toast and butter it and eat it. You make coffee and go to the bottom of the stairs and call up to your mother. "Coffee's ready!" Your neighbor William T. Jones drives by in his pickup and waves. You wave back. The phone rings and you pick it up. You watch yourself doing all these things. You feel as if you are set apart from yourself. Sometimes you think of yourself as *you,* not *I.*

Inside, your heart can barely contain itself from the weight of its aching.

Jimmy Wilson, next to you, isn't looking at you. Jimmy Wilson, next to *me,* isn't looking at *me. It's me, Jimmy, me. Rose. Rose-you've-known-all-your-life Rose.* Warren Graves isn't looking at me either. Katie didn't look at me when I got on. No one's looking at me. I'm invisible. *Hello, I'm Rose Latham. I'm Rose, hello. Can no one talk to Rose anymore? How can you just keep on like this?* I want to scream. *How can you keep living your stupid, stupid lives, when everything is changed?*

Ivy and I had an accident. It was dusk in the Adirondacks that night.

Ivy's sleeping now. I sat by her bed for the past month, waiting for her to wake up. I refused to miss the moment when she woke up.

"I'm not leaving her side," I said to the doctor and the nurse and my mother and William T. "Imagine if she woke up and I wasn't here."

Who else would be there? Not our mother. Our mother works at the Utica Club Brewery all day, and then she drives home, north into the foothills, and spends the evening keeping her fingers busy. So I waited. Waited. Waited.

But she slept. Ivy slept, and slept, and slept. She's still sleeping. And they started chipping away at me. You can't stay here forever, can you, Rose? You need to get back to your routine, don't you? Back to Sterns High, where all your friends are surely missing you, and where you surely must have a ton of work to catch up on. You come down every day after school if you want, they said, but there's nothing to be gained at this point by having you sit by Ivy's bed. The best thing you can do for your sister is to get back to your routine.

How do they know what's best for Ivy?

Jimmy's half-turned around in the seat, talking to Warren. Topic of conversation? The geodesic dome on top of Star Hill. Jimmy sent my mother and me a card after the accident.

"I'm telling you, the CIA owns it," Warren says.

"You've been saying that for as long as I can remember," Jimmy says. "Time to change that channel."

"Mark my words."

Jimmy shakes his head. "It's a former commune. It's a holdover from the sixties. Organic vegetables, et cetera."

"So they would have you think," Warren says. "So they would have the unsuspecting masses think. You're playing right into their hands, Wilson."

How many times in my life have I listened to Warren Graves and Jimmy Wilson talk about the geodesic dome? People like Warren, who believe in conspiracies, are smug. They know better than everyone else. They have access to secret information denied the rest of the world. They are devotees of complexity.

"Chaos complexity," Mr. Carmichael said this morning in science.

He stood at the chalkboard nodding slowly, the way he always does when introducing a new concept. That had not changed in a month either.

"A butterfly flaps its wings in the Amazon rain forest and generates enough wind to create a typhoon in Japan," he said. He was still nodding slowly. "The tiniest of movements on one side of the world sparks something unexpected on the other side. Something unforeseen. Something with consequences undreamt of."

What about a movement that isn't tiny? What about a medium movement, a movement like a blue truck sliding into the car that Ivy and I were driving? What about that action, that consequence?

Ivy and I had an accident. It was dusk in the

Adirondacks that night, and we were coming around a curve.

Jimmy's still half-turned around. Warren's still pontificating about the CIA and the geodesic dome. I want to scream.

"What am I, a moron?" Jimmy says.

"If the shoe fits," Warren says.

Back and forth they go, the way they always go. *Shut up, Warren. Shut up, Jimmy.* Don't they know that everything has changed now? How can they still care about their stupid geodesic dome?

My sister has been without me the entire day. What if today was the day she opened her eyes? What if today was the day she defied the odds, defied the young doctor with the curly brown hair, and opened her eyes the way she did that one time when they said it was just a reflex, and looked around, and I wasn't there? My stomach hurts. I spread my fingers out on my lap. Long and slender. Piano-playing fingers, if we had a piano, which we don't. If my fingers were webbed, I would be a strong swimmer, one of the strongest around. I would be a duck. Duck-girl. Rose the Duck-girl. Rosie the ducky girl, three bucks a peep.

I put my hand on Jimmy Wilson's thigh.

Jimmy's head comes half swiveling back toward me, then he catches himself. He sits still. His entire body is alert. Air before a summer storm, green and electric. I sense it through my fingers, through my palm, which rests on his thigh.

"Hey," Warren says. "Wilson! I'm talking to you! Are you having a seizure? Do I need to put a pencil between your teeth?"

He waves his hand in front of Jimmy's face. "Hellooooo?"

I stroke Jimmy's thigh.

"Wilson!"

"I'm here," Jimmy says.

Beneath my jacket, and behind my backpack, my fingers keep on stroking. This is different. This is something that's changed. I stare out the bus window. Jimmy's house appears.

"See ya," Warren said. "Wouldn't want to be ya."

And Jimmy's gone.

And I'm still sitting on the bus with my arms clasped around my knees, self folded on self: muscle and bone and blood, contained. I am still water. I am water that wants to be a river but is a lake. I am water trapped inside the cage of my body. I am water that wants out. Let me out. Release me.

Ivy and I had an accident. It was dusk in the Adirondacks, and we were coming around a curve. And that was my moment, my moment when time tilted, plucked me up, and set me down again in this unimagined place.

And sometimes every minute is another effort not to scream. Not to scream, and scream, and scream.

My sister knew when I felt this way. My sister knew I hated noise, loud noise, noise that assaulted my ears. She knew I hated the bell at school, that blast of sound that rips through the corridors and halls. Why's it called a bell? Bells ring. Bells chime. Bells are everything that this sound is not.

"What is it with you, Rose?" Ivy said once last year. "You're not some fragile flower."

We were outside, me covering my ears with my hands and cowering: fighter jets taking off from Griffiss Air Base, arrowing into the air faster than sound, spiraling away beyond the foothills.

"They have to *practice,* Rose," Ivy said. "They have to drill themselves in their formations. They have to be prepared."

"PREPARED FOR WHAT?"

My ears were deafened. The only way to communicate was by shouting.

"War, duh. The defending of our homeland against the forces that would overpower it."

And then the sound faded away. Infinitesimal planes too high in the air to see anything but dots streaked higher and higher, chalk lines in their wake. The chalk lines dissolved, began to float, turned themselves into cotton fluff, high in the blue, blue sky.

"Get used to it," Ivy said. "War is noisy, Rosie."

My sister Ivy was the only person in the world who called me Rosie. My sister was the only one in the world who knew how I feel about war, and fighter jets, and the noise they make. "What is it with these people and their wars?" I used to say to Ivy. "World War I, World War II, Korea, Vietnam, the Persian Gulf."

War, war, everywhere. I close my eyes and beam my thoughts to Ivy's hospital bed down in Utica: *Come on, Ivy—wake up. Wake up and call me Rosie.*

If my sister were awake right now, she would take one look at me and say, *It's happening again, isn't it?*

Come on, Rosie, my sister would say. *Let's walk.*

And we would walk. Up the hill that leads to William T.'s house and barn, the broken-down barn where he keeps his flock of lame birds, a left onto Fuller Road, over to Sterns Corners, and then a right past Potato Hill Antiques, and up Potato Hill itself, and then up Star Hill, up the hills and down, through the woods with their green leaves brushing my head, the rutted mud tracks, and back to our house. Walking, walking, miles of walking, the silent screaming surges of electricity calmed and soothed inside the rivers and streams and oceans of my body.

It's late. Dark out. The dishes are done, and my homework is done, and my mother is talking.

"Who knows what they might come up with, Rose? No one knows what's happening out there, who's working on what. They might be able to join nerves together one of these days—take someone whose spinal cord was severed and give him a shot and in an hour or two, he's up and walking."

"Come with me tomorrow," I say. "Come and see her."

If she could see Ivy. If she could see Ivy, Ivy with her hands folded in front of her, Ivy who loved to move, Ivy who used to say, "Come on, Rosie—let's walk."

My mother coils a strand of her hair, lets it spring back, coils another strand, lets it spring back. She's working at her card table. Potholders. She's making potholders.

"You never know what's happening out there," my mother says.

Her fingers work a loop of red through the sea of blue loops already fastened on the pins of the potholder frame. She tugs and pushes and eases the red loop through. Over, under, over, under.

"Did you know that most of our medicine comes from the ground?" my mother says. "Like in the rain forest? Stick a shovel in a patch of dirt that no one's ever stuck a shovel into before, and see what's in there. Check it out. Microorganisms never before seen. Who knows what power they have? They might be able to fix Ivy's brain, stop that hemorrhage, or whatever it is."

She eases another loop of red through the blue. She's so good at it by now that she barely has to look down.

"It's all uncharted territory," she says. "It's all a mystery."

The next day Jimmy Wilson is at my locker.

"Hey, Jimmy."

He has a look on his face, a set look. He keeps looking at me, as if he asked me a question awhile ago and he's getting impatient for the answer. The card he sent me and my mother after the accident had a vase of violets on the front. *Dear Rose and Mrs. Latham,* he wrote on the inside. *I'm very sorry.* Then he had signed his name: *Jimmy W.*

"What's up, Jimmy W.?" I say.

He keeps looking. Waiting. I, too, am waiting. The water that is in me and wants out of me—out, out, out—beats in my veins.

"So what are you doing tonight?" I say.

He shakes his head. He's still waiting.

"I'll tell you what I'm doing," I say. "I plan to skip rocks at the Sterns Gorge. Why not? It'll still be light out."

And that's all it takes.

At twilight I stand on my favorite boulder at the Sterns Gorge, the one I always stand on when I'm skipping rocks, and I skip the last rock from the bunch gathered up in my shirt. I turn around, and there he is. That same set look on his face.

"You scared me," I say. "I couldn't hear you over the water."

"Why did you do that yesterday?"

Right then, I could have stopped. Right at that moment, I could have retreated. Gone back to being Rose, the same Rose that Jimmy Wilson has always known, the one who never responded to his crush because she didn't feel the same way, and she didn't want to hurt him. I could have said what I started to say, which is *I don't know.*

I feel the way I felt just before I put my hand on his thigh, which is *Help me. My body is flying into pieces and I am shards.* Then my hand had spread itself onto his thigh. Had felt Jimmy Wilson's muscles through the worn-out denim of his jeans.

But I don't stop.

"I felt like it," I say. "That's why."

Then I step toward him. He almost backs up, then stops himself. I step again, and again, and then I'm standing against him. We're almost the same height.

I put my hands on his shoulders and tilt my head. He kisses me.

I didn't know it would be so easy. He can hardly

breathe. We're down on the ground in a few minutes, and I'm taking off my clothes. My T-shirt, my jeans, my bra, my underpants. His clothes are gone, too, then he has a condom, then he's lying on top of me, and his breath is coming in gasps, and his eyes are closed.

And it hurts—it hurts—it hurts—and where am I? I'm above, I'm to the side, I'm a tiny untouchable garden with no way in and no way out, and I'm a hovering bird; I'm a fighter jet spiraling away into the foothills, watching what's happening back there on the ground, on that long flat warm rock of the gorge. And then it's over. Jimmy rolls to the side and lies there.

He opens his eyes.

"Rose."

Something in his voice. Something he wants to say to me. His eyes are dark and searching. I get up and put all my clothes back on. I hurt. My body hurts. The hurt feels good; it feels alive—and then that too is gone. I lean over and pick up a rock, a good one, and arc it out with a flick. It skips across the rushing dark water of that tumbling shallow gorge.

Next day there's Jimmy again, standing by my locker.

"Rose."

I'm organizing my books. I've decided that I want the

top shelf of my locker to be a tiny bookcase. A tiny perfect bookcase, organized alphabetically.

"Rose."

"Mmm?"

This must be what it feels like to be a mother, with Jimmy my child and me trying to get dinner on the table while he shoves himself against my legs and whines.

He doesn't say anything.

I can't fit my history book in. It's too tall for the tiny perfect bookcase I'm making out of the top shelf of my locker. It almost fits, but it doesn't. Shove. Get in there, book, you book of wars with your World War I and your World War II and your Korean War and your Vietnam War and your Gulf War and your one after another war and war and war.

What is the matter with these people, these people who won't stop fighting, won't stop hurting each other long enough to see that a body is a thing of beauty, is a miracle of rivers and oceans and islands and continents contained within itself? That the brain is divided into two hemispheres, each symmetrical, each perfect, each with its own system of waterways. These people of war should be shown an x-ray of an intraparenchymal hemorrhage, of a hemorrhage in an eighteen-year-old girl's brain, a girl named Ivy.

Take a look at that, people of war. See, you should not hurt each other, and this is why. Without you ever even trying, this is what can happen to your body, your beautiful body, and your brain, your beautiful symmetrical brain, and your heart, and your soul.

A light blue truck will come sliding toward you without you ever wanting it to, and isn't that enough hurt right there? Isn't that enough? The rivers within me are rising again, flooding over their banks. There is too much inside me, too much to be contained. Get in there, book of wars. Get in there. Stay in there. *Shove.*

Its spine breaks.

"Shit!"

I turn to Jimmy.

"Did you see that?" I say. "I broke the goddamned book."

He's silent. The same look is in his eyes as the day before, when he lay on that huge flat rock looking up at me, and said, "Rose?" Then he turns away.

Wait, Jimmy, I want to say, but I don't.

Wait, little butterfly, flapping your wings in your Amazon rain forest. Please wait. But, too late. The butterfly has flapped his wings and knows not what he has done. Too late, little guy. Too late. Consequences cannot be counted on. That boy behind the wheel of that light blue truck went a little bit fast around that curve, and now a girl who just wants to hear her sister say, *Come on, Rosie—let's walk,* can't. Did those men in my book of wars, those men flying over Hiroshima, have any idea what would happen? Could they ever have imagined what would result when they pushed that button? And when they flew away from what they had done, from what they now could see was happening back there on the ground so far below them, did they feel like me?

CHAPTER TWO

People stare.

Rose-whose-sister-was-in-the-accident. Rose-who-slept-with-Jimmy-Wilson-up-at-the-gorge-did-you-hear?

Rose the freak show.

The corridor swirls with color and sound and motion. I close my eyes and lean against one of the lockers that lines the walls. Feel the hard cool metal. Press into it.

"My mom said she's going to be like that forever. There's no hope."

"Will she end up in a wheelchair?"

"A wheelchair? Are you kidding? She can't even move. She can't eat. She can't even breathe."

"She can't *breathe?*"

"Not without a ventilator. She's a human vegetable. She can't even open her *eyes,* man. She's done for, but they wouldn't pull the plug. That's what my mom said."

The un-bell rings again. That hideous sound that is nothing like a bell is let loose upon the world to do its damage. *Get used to it. War is noisy, Rosie. Open your eyes, Rose. Open your eyes and follow the voices. Around the corner. There.*

"She can open her eyes," I say.

They turn to me. Tracy Benova has a stack of books in one hand. Digging into her locker for her jacket with the other. Todd Forrest with his narrow blue eyes looks away, embarrassed, leans against the locker next to hers.

Tracy's eyes dart back and forth the way they always do when she's about to lie. I know. I've known Tracy Benova all my life. I stand and wait for the Benova lie. I am patient.

"Rose, we were talking about my aunt," Tracy says. "My great-aunt? She's like a thousand years old and she's in a nursing home and she has to be fed through a tube and—"

"You were talking about my sister."

Todd clears his throat. Todd, captain of the debate

team. Todd, Mr. Football. I hold up my hand before he can start talking in that way he talks, like a politician on the television news. *Halt, Mr. Forrest. Cease and desist. You have already lost my vote.*

"And she can open her eyes," I say. "I've seen her open her eyes."

Then there is pressure on my shoulder from behind. I turn, ready to smite the invader. Ready to defend my homeland against the forces that would overpower it.

"Hey."

Tom Miller, his eyes on mine. "Let's go," he says.

He turns me around with the pressure of his hand, and he walks me to my locker with that hand on my shoulder the whole way. I think about saying, *Who the hell do you think you are?* But I'm too tired. And I already know who he is. He's Tom Miller. I've known him, too, all my life. That's how it is when you're born and grow up in the same place, a place where there aren't too many people to begin with. A place like here, in the Adirondacks, where the trees outnumber the people by a thousand to one.

"How is she?" Tom Miller asks.

He stands by my locker as I try to open the combination lock. Why do I even bother locking the stupid locker to begin with? There's nothing of value in it. A rusty barrette, a sandwich left from the day before the accident, so moldy now that it's half dust. A dirty T-shirt. A broken-backed book of wars. Who would want any of this crap?

"How is she?"

Twirl. Twirl. Twirl. Yank. Tom waits. Stupid combination lock. Twirl. Twirl. Twirl. Yank.

"Rose? How's Ivy?"

I shake my head. What can I say to him? Nothing.

Twirl. Twirl. Twirl. Yank.

"Okay," Tom says. "How are *you*?"

Twirl. Twirl. Twirl. Yank.

"Rose."

I do the combination again, exactly right, 11-5-36, and still it won't open. By now I'm late for history and I need the book of wars. Wouldn't want to miss a war, would I? We're up to Korea. Since March the class made its way through the Revolutionary War, the War of 1812, the Civil War, World War I, and World War II. And now it's the end of April, and I'm back in school, and soon we'll be on to Vietnam. Tom Miller's father fought in Vietnam. He fought, and he lived, then he came home, then he kept on living for twelve more years, then he stopped living. Too much Jack Daniel's. Cirrhosis.

"Rose."

Twirl. Twirl. Twirl. Yank. Nothing. Again. Nothing. 11-5-36. Tom's hand again, on my shoulder.

"Shhh," he says.

Am I crying? Yes, I'm crying. Crying, and I'm late

for history, and I still don't have the book of wars, and I don't even want the stupid book of wars, because how many times can you read about Adolf Hitler, and see those black-and-white photos of him and his caterpillar mustache, and see those lines of German soldiers with their goose-stepping, without wanting to reach right into the book and rip him out of there, wring his maniac neck and stop him from doing everything that he and everyone who followed him did? All those naked dead bodies, calling out from their mass graves, their incinerators, their gas chambers. *This is not the world I want to be living in,* I want to scream to that awful, psychotic face of his, barking out all those speeches in German—*this is not the world I want!*

"Shhh. Shhhh."

Tom's looking at me. I've grown up with him. His cousin Joe is Ivy's boyfriend. I've gone to school with Tom from kindergarten on, ridden bikes with him, fished with a string and a safety pin, made plank bridges across Nine Mile Creek, built forts in the haymow. I blow my nose on a piece of notebook paper, which is one of the worst things you can blow your nose on. A dead dried-up leaf is better than a piece of notebook paper. Back to the combination.

11-5-36. Nothing.

11-5-36. Nothing.

Names are being called behind the closed doors of the hall. *Here. Hey. Present. Yo.* Behind the closed door of

Wars, Mr. Trehorn might be calling my name: *Rose Latham?*

Tracy Benova might be raising her hand, wanting to be first with the news. Tracy Benova, bearer of news.

I saw her. I saw her. I saw her in the hall. She's here.

She's not here, though, or she'd be here, right?

I don't know, Tracy might be saying, retreating into Tracyworld. *All I know, Mr. Trehorn, is that she slept with Jimmy Wilson up at the gorge.*

Was Tracy Benova saying that to Mr. Trehorn? No. They were saying it in the hall, though. Did I care? No. I did not care. Why should I? They had called my sister a human vegetable. They were stupid, stupid people.

Twirl. Twirl. Twirl. Yank.

"Rose."

Tom Miller's hand is on my fingers, which are on the combination lock. He pries them off.

"What's the combination?"

"11-5-36."

His fingers twirl the knob. My head hurts. History waits with its wars, down the hall in 107. Tom Miller twirls the knob again. Nothing.

BANG!

He slams the lock against the locker.

BANG!

BANG!

CRACK

It springs open. He pulls the lock free of the door and hands it to me: released.

Later, I sit in the green chair by Ivy's bed. Our neighbor William T. Jones, who lives up the road on top of Jones Hill, sits in the blue chair in the corner behind me. I open up the Pompeii book I checked out in March, when I was planning to do Pompeii for the Destination Imagination project that I'm no longer planning to do.

Let me read to you, Ivy, sister—let me read to you about Pompeii, that lost city.

I lean in close. Hearing is the last to go, is what they say. Somewhere in there, is Ivy listening to me?

"She's not capable of hearing," the doctor said. "She's got no vestibulo-ocular reflex."

But how does he know? Does he know for absolutely sure? Consider the Higgs boson, which was my Destination Imagination project last year. For twenty years, physicists have searched for it. They believe it to be a vibrating chunk of the unseen vacuum that underlies everything in the universe. Can the Higgs boson be seen? No, it cannot. And yet the physicists believe it exists. If the Higgs boson, then why not Ivy's hearing, locked away where no one can find it?

"'On August 24, AD 79,'" I read, "'Pompeii looked like any other busy, prosperous city. People walked the streets of their town, trading goods, news, and friendly talk amongst themselves.'"

"What kind of goods were they trading?" William T. says from behind me, from his blue chair in the corner. "Clay vessels full of olive oil? Flagons of wine, whatever a flagon might actually be?"

His big hands play with my mother's potholders, piled in his lap. He arranges them first in a crisscross pattern, then in a neat stack.

"Potholders, perhaps?"

Every afternoon William T. picks me up after the school bus drops me off at home, and he drives me down here, to the Rosewood Convalescent Home, and after three hours he drives me back to North Sterns. He drops me off at the side door of my house, which is the only door anyone ever uses, including William T. when he comes down the hill to check on us. To make sure that we have enough wood. That we have enough air in our tires. That our furnace isn't going to blow up on us or poison us with carbon monoxide. That we'll live to survive another day.

Sometimes his girlfriend, Crystal, comes with him. She brings us muffins that she makes at her diner, or a container filled with tuna salad. Once she brought a strawberry rhubarb pie that William T. ate half of.

Why does William T. check on us? A long time ago, when my father went away to live in New Orleans, my mother stayed in bed. For weeks. And William T. came to check on us then, and he must've gotten in the habit, because he's never stopped checking on us. Even when his son died five years ago, he still checked on us. See? Awful things happen, and the world just keeps on going. I hate that.

"They didn't have potholders back then, William T.," I say.

"How the hell did they take their pots out of their ovens, then?"

"That's a quarter, William T."

When my mother stayed in bed for that long time and William T. first started coming to check on us, Ivy and I didn't know him very well.

"Girls, I am a man of curse," he said the first time he ever swore in front of us, "but I vow to pay you a quarter every time I curse in front of you."

Damn is allowed, though. In William T.'s opinion, *damn* doesn't qualify as a curse.

"Damn," he says now. "You're right."

Weeks ago, my mother got out the old blue metal potholder loom that William T. gave Ivy and me way back then, back when she stayed in bed for that long time. It's rusty. It doesn't fit together well. It rocks on the table, a lopsided un-square. She strung a row of multicolored nylon loops from one end to the other and began to weave.

My mother's hands are always working. If her hands are stilled, another part of her body is in motion. Her foot, tapping against the floor. Her teeth, grinding lightly against each other. Even her stomach muscles twitch, a rhythm of their own, side to side, if the rest of my mother's body is prevented from movement. Her bones and her muscles show under her skin. She's a body made to move, made for motion. Stillness? No. Never.

Right this very minute, she's making more potholders, up in our house in Sterns.

Over. Under. Over, under. Over under. Overunder-overunderoverunder.

And all the while, she's rocking. Back and forth she rocks, sitting before the card table on her red metal folding chair. She set up the card table a few days after the accident. Once she gets a rhythm going, she increases the speed until she's going as fast as she can. Until her fingers are flying.

My mother works at the Utica Club Brewery, righting tipped bottles of beer. She darts back and forth, plucking up fallen bottles, getting them ready to be boxed. It's a rare bottle left fallen by Connie Latham. If you take the Utica Club Brewery tour, you might be able to see her if you look down from the tour walkway, down onto the assembly floor. The thin woman with dark red hair up in a net, wearing transparent latex gloves? The one who drives the rusting red Datsun parked at the far end of the employee parking lot? The one who won't look up and catch your eye? That's her. You'll watch the line of bottles pass before her disorderly and emerge in order. Maybe you'll wonder about her: How old is she? Is she married? Does she have children?

Forty-three.

No.

Two, daughters both: Rose and Ivy.

Or maybe you'll look down and see her, and you won't wonder anything at all about her, about this woman, this Connie Latham, Employee of the Month three years ago in February, this woman righting tipped bottles on the conveyor belt, machinery clanging all about her.

My mother has not been to see Ivy since they moved her here from the hospital.

At home her foot taps out a rhythm to a song I can't hear, a song inside her head. What if the brewery were to shut down? What would my mother do then? My mother needs motion, constant movement, and she also needs structure, a set rhythm to contain that movement, the way moving water needs the banks of a river in order to keep itself from overflowing and disappearing into the ground.

"Water seeks its own level," Mr. Carmichael said in science last year. He stood at the map of the world, pointing out threads of blue winding their way through vast fields of green. "Look at them. The Tigris, the Euphrates, the Mississippi, the Amazon, the Yangtze. The world's great rivers. And every one of them finds its way to the ocean."

William T. dangles one of my mother's potholders in the air by its little loop.

"How the hell do you know they didn't trade potholders back in the days of Vesuvius, Younger?" he says. "Did they just walk around with burned hands all the time?"

Elder and Younger, William T.'s renames for Ivy and me from back in the time when my mother stayed in bed.

"Think of the killing I could've made if I lived back then," he says. "I would have had a potholder stand in the marketplace. I would have been known as King of the Potholders, however you say that in ancient Greek."

"Latin," I say. "Pompeii was part of the Roman Empire."

William T. shakes his head.

"And that right there, Younger," he says, "is why you are an honor roll *habituée* and I, a mere potholder king."

"'Three days after the volcano erupted, all sounds of life had fallen silent, and Pompeii itself had vanished. Almost nothing was seen of Pompeii for more than 1,500 years, and only now, more than 1,900 years later, are we learning more about its last days. During the first eight hours of the eruption of Vesuvius, eight feet of dust and ashes and cinders and rocks fell on Pompeii. Roofs collapsed from the heaps of small rocks. Next, a boiling cloud of steam and mud flowed down the side of Vesuvius and covered the town of Herculaneum.'

"And what can we see today of Pompeii?" I say to Ivy. "Naught but ruins."

Before the accident, when I was still planning to do Pompeii for my Destination Imagination project, I had planned to write a story about an ordinary Pompeian family on the last day of their lives.

I imagined a Pompeii woman standing before a clay oven where bread was baking. A baby in a rush basket slept in a corner. Sun streamed through a narrow slit window in a thick clay wall. The woman glanced at the baby: yes, still asleep. She could sit and close her eyes for a moment. She had time.

"Damn," William T. says. The loop has become unknotted and the potholder is coming apart, unweaving itself.

"You little devil of a potholder, you," he says. "Stay together."

More loops unweave themselves. The potholder wants to return to its original state: long loops at rest, unstretched, untwisted.

"I command thee, potholder," William T. says, "to stay together. Look at this thing, Younger. It's trying to commit potholder hari-kari."

William T. looks up from the potholder and grins. He has a beautiful grin. Without guile. Without anything other than grin in it.

Angel, the nurse who wears a different angel pin every day, pushes open the door. Her name isn't really Angel. Her real name, according to the name tag she wears just below her angel pin, is Dorothy Van Gulden. But William T. took one look at her angel pin the first day he met her and renamed her Angel. She picks up Ivy's chart and gazes at the ventilator screen and makes a few notes. The sound of the ventilator pushing air into my sister's lungs is the softest sound in the world. Angel puts down the chart and strokes Ivy's hair. That's her ritual.

"What's the bird of the day, William T.?" she says.

That's another of her rituals. While William T. sits behind me, in the blue chair in the corner, he studies his bird book. William T. uses his Rosewood Convalescent Home free time wisely, improving his knowledge of the birds of North America.

"I'll give you a hint, Angel," William T. says. "The bird of the day is a long-winged, very fast-flying relative of the shearwater."

"Oh dear. I've never even heard of a shearwater, so how could I possibly know any of its relatives?"

"Angel. How the hell can you call yourself a birder when you've never heard of a shearwater?"

"I don't," Angel says. "I've never called myself a birder."

William T. shakes his head.

"Your loss, then. The bird of the day is a relative of

the shearwater, and it's found one hundred to two hundred miles off the California coast. Give me your best guess."

He waits. That's part of their ritual. Angel pretends to think hard.

"A chickadee?"

"A *chickadee*? Jesus."

"Some kind of offshore water bat?"

"*Offshore water bat?* Is there such a thing?"

"Anything's possible," Angel says.

"Except for offshore water bats," William T. says. "Do you give up?"

She nods. Every day, Angel gives up.

"The bird of the day," William T. says, "is a deep-water petrel."

She nods appreciatively, just as she does every day, and turns back to Ivy. She rubs Ivy's feet. She smoothes Ivy's hair off her forehead. Ivy's face is beautiful. Perfect. You would never know to look at her how badly hurt the inside of her head is. Angel touches Ivy's cheek, and then she turns to go. William T. salutes her as if he's a soldier and she, his commanding officer. That's the last part of their ritual. She smiles at him.

"At ease, William T.," Angel says, and the door closes behind her.

CHAPTER THREE

Ivy and I had an accident. It was dusk in the Adirondacks that night, and we were coming around a curve. And Ivy pumped the brakes, but a light blue truck was going too fast, and it came sliding into us.

It's still happening.

Some mornings I wake and the sun glimmers over the pines across the road, and it's another day, and I love the days, I love waking up, but something's wrong—something's wrong—something—

Oh.

The accident won't stop happening. Over and over it

happens, and I would give anything to have my sister back.

You would? I hear Ivy saying. *What, exactly, would you give up, Rosie?*

My sister knew how much the idea of sacrifice intrigues me. Stories of the martyrs and saints. I used to like to put myself through periods of austerity. Giving up hot water when showering. Dessert for Lent. Extra sleep on school vacation days, my electric blanket on cold winter nights.

"I'm testing myself," I used to tell Ivy. "Good preparation for life's future hurdles."

When we were little, I dragged a few of William T.'s old truck tires into the woods and laid them one in front of the other.

"This is an obstacle course," I told Ivy. "In order to get the highest rating, you must leap from the center of one tire to the center of the next tire, never slowing, never stopping. Points will be taken off if I detect a look of tiredness on your face."

But Ivy wouldn't play.

"You are such a weirdo," she said.

I used to do my obstacle course by myself. Ivy stood by the side laughing at me.

"Yikes!" she would say. "Do I detect a look of tiredness on your face? Indeed, I do. One point off."

Ivy didn't like to sacrifice. She didn't believe in it.

"Life is short, little sister," she said. "Take advantage."

Sometimes I would wake in the night to the sound of hail. Joe Miller, Ivy's boyfriend, standing in the darkness, tossing pebbles at Ivy's window. And Ivy would go with him, jumping into his truck that idled by the side of the road, lights off.

Joe Miller was not a welcome presence at Sterns High. Teachers were glad to see him go when he graduated last year. Now he works at Gray's Automotive in Remsen, with all the other Millers. He used to roar down Jones Hill after work, steer fast into the driveway so that bits of gravel spewed from under his tires, and come swinging down from the driver's seat, the truck still running, and bound up the steps to the kitchen door. *Knock, knock.* "Hey, Mrs. Latham. Hey there, Rose. What's on the sacrifice menu today?"

Like my mother, Joe Miller has not been to see Ivy since they moved her from the hospital to the Rosewood Convalescent Home.

You could almost see something in the air between Ivy and Joe. Something in Joe Miller's body, and something in Ivy's, drew them to each other. Maybe they knew each other in a former life. Maybe they walked a dusty road together, a dusty road in the desert, and they held hands, and when they stopped to rest, maybe Joe-in-the-former-life held Ivy's foot between his hands and rubbed the tiredness out of her muscles while they talked softly between themselves. It's possible. "Anything's possible," said Angel. "Except for offshore water bats," said William T.

I can hear Ivy now.

What, exactly, would you give up to get me back, Miss Sacrifice? Be specific.

Is there anything I would not give up?

Ivy was behind the wheel, and I was next to her. We rounded the curve. We saw the truck. The boy's light blue truck. Ivy pumped the brakes. The truck slid gently into our car.

And that was my moment, my moment when time tilted, plucked me up, and set me down again here, in this unimagined place.

"Your sister can't hear you," the doctor said. "She has no vestibulo-ocular reflex."

But there's more to this world than meets the eye, isn't there? That same doctor might say to a man whose leg is missing: "Your leg's not there anymore. It can't hurt you." It does, though. Ever heard of phantom pain, Mr. Smart-doctor-who-thinks-he-knows-everything-but-doesn't?

Would you give up sugar to get me back, Rosie? You know you love sugar.

Of course I would give up sugar, Ivy.

Easily. No candy bars, sourballs, oatmeal butterscotch cookies, Boston cream pie, or carrot cake with cream cheese frosting. No chocolate either. No maple syrup or honey. Cough drops even. Goodbye to you, sugar. Goodbye and good riddance. A sacrifice, but enough of a sacrifice?

No. You can't get me back that easily. What else?

Bike riding. I would give up bike riding for you, Ivy.

No more riding down Jones Hill, no more wind blowing back my hair, no more crisscrossing Route 274 after the sun's gone down and it's just me and the stars in the dark night sky. No more *wishhh* of tires on pavement, no more looking back once to make sure that the kitchen light's still on before I forge on up the road, the moon ever brighter, the air ever cooler. Goodbye to bike riding.

A sacrifice, but not enough of a sacrifice. Aren't I worth more than that? Come on. What else?

Driving. I would give up driving to get you back, Ivy.

Ha! That's not a sacrifice! You don't even know how to drive.

The people of Pompeii never had to learn to drive. They never came around a curve in the road one night in March, in the hills where they lived, to find a light blue truck sliding toward them, coming straight at them. Somebody from Gray's Automotive, someone who wasn't Joe Miller, towed our car away from the accident and took it down to Utica, where they crushed it into a lump of scrap metal.

Ivy is right; I don't drive. Why not?

Because.

Because Ivy and I had an accident. It was the end of winter, dusk in the Adirondacks, and we came around a curve. And then Ivy wasn't moving, and she wasn't answering, and was she breathing? Blood. My window was broken and I broke it more. I punched it with my jacket wrapped around my hand, punched and punched, and I crawled out and fell up. We were upside down? How had that happened? I ran. I ran, and ran, and ran, and ran, pavement and patchy March ice, until I came to the cabin on Deeper Lake where Tom Miller lives with his grandfather Spooner.

"Hello?"

Tom's voice.

I tried to scream but there was only a wheeze, a whisper. I staggered up Tom's sand driveway, and Tom was standing there with a bucket of water and a flashlight.

"Rose?"

Light, shining in my face. Blinding me. It swung crazily away and Tom was yelling.

"Grampa! She's bleeding!"

His grandfather, old Spooner, came bursting from the cabin, a red dish towel clutched in his hand. I saw the truck and I was on it, tugging at its rusted door, trying to yank it open.

"What's going on?" Spooner said. "She's bleeding. Who is she?"

"Rose Latham," Tom said.

I was in the truck and turning the key, and there was a scraping sound—metal on metal, a hurting scraping sound—and Spooner yelled.

"It's a stick! Push the clutch in!"

But I didn't know how to drive.

Then they were both in the truck with me, Tom riding on the hump and me crawling over him so Spooner could put it in reverse, wheel around, and head down their long curving sand driveway to 274.

"We had an accident," I said. "We were coming around a curve. Ivy's still in there."

Spooner behind the wheel was making the truck fly like it couldn't ordinarily do. I could tell from the shuddering and shaking. The whole side of my face was pressed into the glass, my body rocking forward and back as if I were part of the truck, part of what made us swoop around the curves that led into the mountains from the foothills. My ears popped. Someone was saying something to me, but I was gone into another world, a world of rocking with my back and hips, a world of forcing the truck forward with my palms flattened on the glass.

All it takes is a single moment. Think about your own life. Something happened once—a door opened the wrong way, maybe, or an expression you never saw before appeared on the face of your father, or your dog ran toward the road, or your mother raised her hand, or a black bird hovered high in the sky above you—and suddenly you're running, you're running in the foothills, running for help, and you can't get your breath, and you can't get your breath, and you can't—get your breath—and you *can't—get—your—breath—*

Jimmy Wilson sits a few seats up, next to Warren Graves. All of us are silent, staring out at the green, all the shades of green that are an Adirondacks May in North Sterns. Jimmy's whole body is rigid with his not-looking at me. I look at his rigid not-looking-at-Rose-Latham head and I remember the way his body went rigid for a second up at the gorge, and the way he looked at me the next day at my locker. I don't want to think about Jimmy Wilson, but there he is with his head not turning around, and that head of his is all I can see.

Then Warren stands up. You aren't supposed to stand up while the bus is in motion, and you're supposed to stay behind the line when the bus is in motion, and you aren't supposed to walk down the aisle, all the way back to where I'm sitting, alone and trapped on my green vinyl seat, and you aren't supposed to slide into the seat next to me, slide so close that your leg is touching my leg, is pressing against my thigh, and you aren't supposed to stare at me like this, the way that Warren's staring at me.

He doesn't blink.

I feel his stare. I feel the others staring. They sit rigid

in their seats and some of their heads are pressing together and some of their mouths are moving, are whispering, are talking about Ivy Latham. Ivy who would not be in a wheelchair, Ivy who can't *breathe,* who's a human *vegetable.* I listen intently so that I'll know who's saying what, so that I can push my way past the staring Warren and set them straight about my sister.

But they're not talking about Ivy. They're talking about me, Rose Latham, Rose and Jimmy. *Who knew, who knew, who knew, who would ever have thought—I mean, Rose? Rose Latham?*

"Isn't that right, Wilson?" Warren calls, as if he's said something to Jimmy, which he hasn't.

Way up near the front of the bus, Jimmy Wilson doesn't turn around.

"Isn't that RIGHT?" Warren calls again.

I zero in on Warren, next to me. I can feel his thoughts. He thinks he has the right—he can stare at me all he wants, he can press his leg against mine as hard, hard, hard as he wants, and I won't protest. He thinks he has something on me and that I won't say anything. He thinks I'm ashamed.

Wrong.

He and the hall-talkers and the bus-talkers are wrong. They think they know what happened up at the gorge with me and Jimmy, but they don't. They don't know that sometimes the world should stop for a while, but it doesn't. Jimmy Wilson's body on mine hurt—it hurt—but it was a different kind of hurt from the hurt that comes from Ivy lying on that bed and not waking up.

"Right, Wilson? Rose is going to skip some stones with me at the gorge tonight."

Jimmy's head stays rigid.

"Sure," I say. "Sounds like fun."

For just a second, Warren looks surprised. Then he recovers.

"Okay, Rosie. See you later, then."

Rosie. That, I was not prepared for. That, I had no defense against. My sister, Ivy, was the only one who called me Rosie.

"What time, Rosie?"

I stand up and push past him, push past his legs that are blocking my way. Down the aisle I go. Can't see. Can't see. Behind me I hear Warren saying, "What? What? What did I say, Rosie?" *Do not call me Rosie.* I'm trying to keep my balance with my hand, seat to seat. Down the aisle I go until I come to Katie and I can't go any farther, and I sit down in front of the stay-behind-the-line-when-the-bus-is-in-motion. On the floor next to Katie, my legs braced against the steps that lead down and out.

"Hey!" Katie says. "You can't sit here. Get the hell back there and sit your butt down."

Can't see. Can't see.

"NOW."

Back I go. Behind the line I go, while the bus is in motion. There's an empty seat. Drop into it. No, this is Jimmy Wilson's seat. Too late. Jimmy doesn't look at me. His head stays rigid. Behind us, Warren.

"What? What? What did I say? Geez!"

And then we're at my house, and Katie chuffs off in a cloud of tired blue exhaust. I'm inside my house, my house where my sister isn't. *It's happening again, isn't it, Rosie? Come on—let's walk.*

CHAPTER FOUR

"All Millers go through crazy," William T. says when I tell him how Tom broke my lock for me.

"They aren't meant to stay in school," he says. "You can see it in them from kindergarten on. Millers go through crazy and a bunch of them stay there."

Crazy. As if it were a geographical location. A place that's on the way to another place, a stopover on a trip, a town, or a tourist destination, Crazy with a capital C.

"Tom Miller's not crazy," I say.

William T. considers. I can see him turning Millers over in his mind, beginning with Joe and moving on to

Greg and Tubes and Shorty and ending with Spooner. *No,* I can see him thinking, *Spooner's not crazy, at least not in a Miller way—and Tom, being Spooner's grandson, might well not be crazy, either, at least not in that Miller way.*

"You might be right, Younger," he says after a while. "Tom Miller might be the Miller exception who proves the Miller rule."

I once watched Tom Miller in the school hallway, like a beautiful young horse, muscle and thirst, bend over the drinking fountain and drink. He drank and drank and drank, as if he could never get enough.

"Tom's father was crazy, though," William T. says. "Even before the war, Chase Miller was a little bit crazy."

Chase Miller had gone to Vietnam, to the jungle. Vietnam is the next war in our book of wars. When I try to picture the jungle there, I see color: green of trees, brown of bark, plants growing to the heavens because there's no end to the sun and the rain and the warmth. Neon parrots squawking in the trees, snakes coiled around tree limbs. As far away from here as I can imagine a place being.

"That goddamned war did Chase in," William T. says.

I don't say, *You owe me a quarter, William T.*

Chase died of cirrhosis before Tom was born, and Tom's mother couldn't take it and she left him with Spooner.

"She moved to Canada," William T. told me once. "To get away from the sickness of America, she said."

Tom's always lived with his grandfather Spooner, in their log cabin on Deeper Lake. No electricity. No running water. You can walk to Deeper Lake from my house. You can walk anywhere in the world from my house. You might have to cross uncharted mountains, you might have to walk underwater for thousands of miles to get across the ocean, but, if you are determined enough, you can walk anywhere in the world from my house. You can walk to the jungles of Vietnam and lose yourself there.

I open the blinds and let the sunlight into Ivy's room. May air is soft and sweet through the screened window. William T. sits in his blue chair, reading his bird book and expanding his knowledge of the birds of America. If Ivy and I hadn't had our accident, William T. would be helping his girlfriend, Crystal, close her diner for the night. Right about now, Crystal is scraping down the grill. If William T. were at Crystal's Diner, he would be wiping down each of the red counter stools in turn. Then he would turn to the booths and scrub each wooden tabletop and each red vinyl seat. By the time he was finished, Crystal would be finished prepping for tomorrow morning's breakfast. They would leave together and get into Crystal's truck or William T.'s truck, whoever had driven that day. Before the accident, I sometimes used to help them. Fill the sugar containers. Fill the salt and pepper shakers. Make sure there was plenty of ketchup in the ketchup bottles. Lots of people like ketchup with their eggs, did you know that? I didn't, before I used to help out Crystal and William T.

Now William T. spends his afternoons in the blue chair, putting his time to good use while I read to Ivy.

Angel comes in on her silent sneakered feet. Her angel pin is at her waist today, a small change of pace.

"Angel, I have a question for you."

"And what is your question, William T.?"

"It's a concentration camp question."

Angel doesn't miss a beat. She never misses a beat. She's like Crystal that way, takes William T. just as he is, concentration camp question and all.

"You're in a concentration camp being given your ration for the day," William T. says. "Three pieces of bread and one pat of butter."

"Butter in a concentration camp, William T.? I think you've got your history wrong."

"Don't be so literal, Angel. Use your imagination. Your ration for the day is three pieces of bread and one small pat of butter."

"And?"

"And, how do you eat the butter? Do you (a) spread it thickly on one piece of bread and eat the other two plain?, (b) spread it on all three pieces, evenly but so thinly that you can barely taste it?, or (c) save the small pat of butter and add it to the other days' small pieces of butter until the end of the week, so that you can have three pieces of bread all spread very thickly with butter?"

Angel tilts her head, considering the possibilities of butter and bread in the concentration camp. Deep in thought.

"Ha!" William T. says. "It's a trick question. I already know how you'd eat it."

"How would I, then?"

"B. Spread on all three pieces, evenly but so thinly that you can barely taste it."

"You're right! That *is* how I'd eat it. Are you psychic, William T.? Tell the truth."

"I am," William T. says. "I cannot lie. I already know how Younger here would eat it too. Younger would save her little lumps of butter all week long. And then she'd spread her three pieces of bread with an inch of butter, and eat them all at once. I'm right, aren't I, Younger?"

Yes. He's right.

"Do I get the bird of the day free, as a bonus?" Angel asks.

"Indeed you do, Angel. The bird of the day is the black-capped chickadee."

"A chickadee? Did you choose that just for me, William T.?"

"Perhaps," William T. says. "Perhaps I did."

He and Angel smile. They like to flirt with each other.

It's safe flirting, because Angel loves her husband and William T. loves Crystal. I don't flirt with anyone. I don't know how to flirt, unlike Ivy, who flirted with Joe Miller all the time. Are some people just born knowing how?

"'Little roving flocks of black-capped chickadees,'" William T. reads from his bird book, "'are often the brightest spark of life in bleak winter woods.'"

Outside Ivy's window the bleak winter is gone. The grass is green now, so much greener than when they first moved Ivy here in the beginning of April. That makes me angry. Grass, how can you be so green, when my sister can't see you? Stop. Stop being so beautiful, so alive, so goddamned green. Stop growing. Stupid, idiot, beautiful grass.

William T. was with me when the doctor showed me the x-ray.

"It's an enormous intraparenchymal hemorrhage," the doctor said. "She cannot recover from this."

"But she was talking to me," I said to the doctor. "She was talking to me, right after it happened."

"Yes," he said. "The swelling hadn't yet taken over. We call that the lucid interval."

She was almost brain-dead but not quite. That's what they said. She didn't open her eyes; she didn't move her eyes when they opened them for her and brushed them with the cotton swab; she didn't gag; she didn't look toward the ice water in her ear. They turned the ventilator off and we waited.

Waited.

Waited.

Waited.

And she tried to breathe.

"She has a very slight respiratory drive," they said. "But you must understand: she will never recover from the brain trauma."

Then the woman with the curly hair came into the waiting room and asked about Ivy's heart. Ivy's liver. Ivy's kidneys.

"No," my mother said.

And so they kept Ivy alive. My mother couldn't let her go.

Could I have let her go? If someone asked me to make the decision instead of my mother—*Tell us what to do: keep your sister's heart beating or let her go*—what would I have said? My mother's face was set, the way it gets sometimes. She doesn't let anything behind that face. She listens to no one. She's a wall. If you stood on the walkway above the conveyor belt on the floor of the brewery, looking down at my mother darting back and forth, righting the fallen bottles, you wouldn't know that about her.

"No," my mother said. "No."

Her hands were over her ears at that point.

When I think of my sister Ivy, my heart aches. My

heart aches, my heart that is contracting and pumping in my chest right now, contracting and pumping, pushing and pulling my blood, my rich red blood, throughout the rivers and islands and gorges of my body.

Doctors could take away my sister's heart and put it inside someone else's chest, and connect all the tubes and stitch it up and prescribe medicine to make the strange person not reject my sister's heart, not reject it, not say, *What the hell is this, this thing, this unfamiliar thing beating away inside my chest,* and, *Get the hell out of here.* And my sister's heart would keep that person alive.

But where would Ivy be? Sometimes I think about that. It's a mystery. It's an unknown world. I think about the Higgs boson that opens the door to another, as yet completely undiscovered, realm. When I studied the Higgs boson for my project, I read that only 4 percent of the universe is made up of atoms with known forces, such as gravity and electromagnetism, the ordinary stuff that makes water and rocks and potholders and scalpels. The other 96 percent is dark matter. Dark energy. And no one knows what dark matter and dark energy are.

"No," my mother said. "No. You can't understand. I can't lose her."

That's what I remember from the night of the accident, after Tom and Spooner and William T. and Crystal—where did they come from?—got us to the hospital. Ahead of the ambulance.

Fluorescent lights. A long tiled hallway. People dressed in blue, people dressed in white, standing in a circle around my mother.

"No," she said.

They turned to me when my mother stopped listening, when she put her hands over her ears.

"Your father?"

That's how they said it, as if they had already figured out that *your father* wasn't part of the picture. As if there were a single-word multiple-choice question.

Father? Check all that apply:

___ Missing in action

___ Hasn't seen wife or daughters in nine years

___ Living in New Orleans last we heard

I shook my head. No. The one doctor had a look of frustration on his face, and he turned back to my mother.

"No," she said.

Eventually everyone disappeared, and my mother was alone under those fluorescent lights. That's what I remember, even though I know that William T. and Crystal and Spooner and Tom Miller and I were there too. I still can see my mother's face that night, the way her cheeks hollowed under the long ribbons of fluorescence. After a while William T. reached out and placed his hands over her hands over her ears and gently pulled them down.

"Home, Younger?" William T. asks me once we're in the truck, headed north.

I shake my head. I don't want to watch my mother rocking and listen to her not talking about Ivy. It tires me out, the effort it takes not to talk about Ivy.

"Eggs, then?"

I nod. And we drive past my driveway, past the house where my mother is home from the brewery, and on up Jones Hill to William T.'s house. Back in North Sterns, back from Ivy's room, back from Angel and her concentration camp bread and butter and the black-capped chickadee bonus bird of the day.

William T.'s making me scrambled eggs the way he makes them for me. Slow and patient, that's his method. Other people can make scrambled eggs in one-quarter the time it takes William T. to make them. But other people's scrambled eggs taste nothing like William T.'s. He makes them for me quite a bit, whenever I'm up at his house. Which is more and more.

"You were right," I say. "About the way I'd eat the bread and butter."

"Of course I was right," he says. "I know my Younger."

"William T.?"

"Younger?"

"What was my father like?"

"Your father?"

"Yeah. My father."

I wait. William T. pours the eggs into the hot butter in his special egg pan.

"He was a man of bad decisions."

It sounds as if he's read a book and memorized it for the day when I would come to him, asking about my father. *Fathers of North America.* Who else can I ask? Not my mother. Since that time, that long time when she stayed in bed, neither Ivy nor I have said a word to her about our father.

A man of bad decisions. Okay. I wait.

"Yes," William T. says, as if I've asked a question when I haven't. "Bad decisions."

Sometimes William T. makes eggs for me in my own house, when he comes down to check on my mother. My mother is not big on food in general, but she'll eat William T.'s scrambled eggs. William T. shakes his head.

"Not good choices," he says.

Not good choices. A variation on the theme of bad decisions. Okay. I wait.

"What do you want to know exactly, Younger?" he says, finally. I knew that if I waited long enough, even William T. wouldn't be able to bear the silence. Like most people, he would want to fill it with words. Most people hate silence. They want to fill it, cover it up, make it go away. Down with silence, and its endless unspoken questions.

"Anything I can."

"He lives down in Louisiana, last I heard. He went down there after he left Sterns."

"No winters in Louisiana," I observe.

William T. stirs the scrambled eggs. Around and around he stirs with his wooden egg-stirring spoon. The flame is so low you can barely see it, tiny blue tongues licking the bottom of the cast-iron pan. I sit on the stool and watch him. Finally he speaks again.

"Younger, the thing about your father is that he didn't like himself in his natural state."

Okay—

"He preferred a little embroidery on his reality. Let's put it that way."

Okay—

"He loved your mother. I know that he loved her—you could see it. But he loved that embroidered reality more."

Okay—

But what about me and Ivy? Did our father love us too?

The eggs are finished. Quivering pillows of buttery yellow. William T. spoons them onto a saucer instead of a plate. He knows I like to eat them from a small saucer rather than a big plate, and with a spoon rather than a fork. I picture my father, a young man in Louisiana. Lying on his back in the middle of a small park in New Orleans. I saw a picture of such a park once.

"If he's not dead," William T. says, "then he's almost forty years old."

In my mind, jazz musicians play softly about him. Tourists with hot beignets from a hot beignet store wander by, powdered sugar drifting down upon my father like the snow he left behind.

"Imagine that," William T. says. "Forty years old. Time marches on, doesn't it, Younger?"

He wipes his special egg pan dry with a dish towel and shakes his head. Forty years old. I don't even know what my father looks like.

"They're talking about Ivy in school," I say.

I didn't know I was going to say that. William T. stiffens the same way that Jimmy Wilson does whenever he sees me now, unlike Warren, who after I lay down with him at the gorge that night just looks at me with a lazy, knowing look. And smiles. A lazy, knowing smile that I hate. But given the choice between Jimmy Wilson's rigid not-looking at me, I will take Warren Graves's knowing smile. William T. looks at me with searching eyes.

"They're talking about Elder?"

"They are."

"What are they saying?"

"That she's a human vegetable. That she can't open her eyes. That she'll be like this forever. That she's only alive because my mother won't let them pull the plug."

Words, tumbling out. Tracy Benova and Todd Forrest, standing together at Tracy's locker. Bits and pieces of other people's conversations.

William T. is quiet. I watch his face. All I see is sadness. After a while he picks up his truck keys and clears his throat.

"You ready, Younger?"

"No."

The egg pan is dried and put away; the sun has set. It's time, but I don't want it to be time.

"Your mother needs you."

"My mother doesn't visit her own daughter."

William T. looks at me. I see his mind at work. He wants to say something, but he doesn't know how to say it.

"Well, she doesn't," I say when he keeps looking at me with that look on his face. "You know it as well as I do."

"Don't underestimate your mother, Younger," he says, which is what he always, finally, says.

Every night I watch my mother's fingers moving. She can't keep still. She, too, is moving water that wants to keep moving. She's like the cascading water of the Sterns Gorge, dipping and eddying around rocks. Once in a while you can find a pool by the side of the bank, a still, deep pool where the water rests before giving in again to the tumble. On the hottest summer days, I sometimes lower myself into that pool. Spread my arms on the surrounding rocks and hang there, suspended. Cold seeps through my skin, cools my entire body. The top of my head is warm from the sun, and the rest of me cools and cools and cools until suddenly, I'm cold, and then too cold, and I haul myself out and lie on that long flat rock and wait for the sun to warm me again.

Would I give up the Sterns Gorge to get my sister back, back the way she used to be?

I would give it up. Goodbye, my rock and my water rushing by, so busy, so full of purpose, rushing by on your way, on your way to where you're going. I give you up willingly, that I may have my sister back.

"Your mother doesn't have an easy time of it," William T. says, which is something else that he always says.

What I want to say is, *Who does? Who the hell does have an easy time of it?* Not Ivy. Not Ivy, who lies in bed with her eyes closed, the ventilator pushing air into her lungs through her tracheotomy, the faintest of sounds: *wishhh, wishhh, wishhh.*

Not my mother, whose fingers are always in motion. "You have no idea how noisy it is inside here," she said once to Ivy and me, and pointed at her head.

But I do. I do know. I know all about noise and electricity, silent screams running up and down the waterways of my body. I know about walking, rhythm, the cadence of footsteps that tire my muscles and bring me peace, bring me peace, bring me peace.

"I try not to think," my mother said in her Utica Club Brewery Employee of the Month interview. "The less I think, the better I am at my job."

She's good at her job. She should be; she's been at the brewery more than twenty years.

All my life my mother's hands have talked for her. Look down at her from the tour walkway, down on the assembly floor. See her thin hands as she rights the fallen and tipped bottles. See how graceful and quick they are. At night sometimes, when I was little, before the long time when my mother stayed in bed, I would wake to feel her hands on my forehead, stroking, stroking, stroking back my hair.

"I like to work hard and be all tired out," she told the interviewer. "Keeps me out of trouble."

Give her a garden and she'll weed it. Give her a barbed-wire fence and she'll fix it. Give her a sinkful of dirty dishes and she'll wash them. Give her a pile of laundry and she'll fold it.

Give her a daughter in a hospital bed and what does she do?

Nothing.

My Pompeii book, in my backpack, is two months overdue. Silently I read to myself, there at William T.'s kitchen table. I read about Pliny the Elder, who witnessed the disaster at Pompeii. He saw the thick black cloud advancing behind him like a flood. He heard women shrieking, children crying, and men shouting.

William T. stands up and stretches his arms above his head, the sure sign that I have to go now. That it's time.

"They're saying that she wouldn't pull the plug," I say.

"That's true."

"She won't let her go, but she won't visit her either."

"Your mother does the best she can."

"William T.?"

"Younger?"

"Can you pick me up at school from now on?"

He regards me. I can see the questions chasing themselves around in his brain.

Why does Younger want me to pick her up? Does she not want to take the bus? Did something happen on the bus? Should I ask her if something's wrong? No, because so much is wrong that she wouldn't even be able to answer such a stupid question.

If William T. asks me about the bus, will I be able to keep quiet about Jimmy and Warren and the gorge? I watch him and will him just to say *yes.*

"Yes," he says.

"Thank you."

And he drives me back down the hill to where my mother is sitting and rocking and not talking about Ivy.

CHAPTER FIVE

I rise in the early morning and walk into the kitchen in my bare feet. The floor is wooden. Be careful. Step lightly on the old boards. Splinters.

Make the coffee. Pour it into the daffodil mug and add the cream and stir in the sugar and bring it upstairs. Give it to Mom. On Thursdays she doesn't go into work until nine.

"Here you go, Mom."

And out the door I go. School. At 8:10 the un-bell will rip its way out of the speakers to find release in the corridors and hallways of Sterns High. No more un-bell for me. No more noise that splits my ears. No more bus. No more green vinyl seats. No more Katie the bus driver telling me to *get the hell back there and sit your butt down.* No more Jimmy, who won't look at me anymore, and no more Warren, who will.

I walk.

I time my walk to get there after the un-bell has shrieked. In time for science, and history, and trigonometry, and the looks, and the silences, and the whispers.

Before I start my walk, I turn around and look up William T. Jones's hill toward his white house and his broken-down barn. William T. is probably at his girlfriend Crystal's diner, where he goes every morning. He meets his friend Burl Evans there for breakfast, and Crystal pours them both coffee, and William T. organizes the jam packets in their holders. I beam my thoughts to William T., sitting on his stool at the counter at Crystal's Diner: *Hi, William T. I'm off. I'll see you this afternoon. Don't be late.*

That's my good-luck ritual.

What if I tell him what I did last night, when the still water rose within me, overflowed its banks, and I walked to the gorge because I had to go to the gorge, and Todd Forrest was there, and he asked if he could kiss me, too, and I said I didn't care and he put his arms around me and picked me up and he asked if he could unzip my jeans and I said I didn't care and he had a condom, too, and he asked and I said I didn't care and then it was happening again and it hurt again and stone was beneath me, stone all around me, the rushing water that I want to *be* rushing behind me where I couldn't see it, flowing fast and free over more stone. I closed my eyes until it was over, and then I lay there and it was Ivy I saw, Ivy, silhouetted against the moon, standing in the paneless window of the hay barn.

No. I can't tell William T. about that. What would I say?

William T., help. I'm in trouble.

No.

What I do instead is walk. I walk, and most days, before I get to the intersection of Crill Road and 274, the rhythm of walking is upon me. My brain relays signals through the nerve pathways of my body, and my feet do their bidding. Unlike Ivy's brain, which doesn't work anymore. When the doctor showed me that x-ray of Ivy's brain, I didn't think it looked so bad. Fuzzy, gray, a few faint blurry lines here and there. Isn't that what an ordinary brain looks like? The doctor stood there, gazing at Ivy's brain, and I stood there gazing too.

"That's what an intraparenchymal hemorrhage looks like, Miss Latham."

The doctor nodded slowly, and I nodded too.

Then he put up an x-ray of a normal brain. It too was fuzzy and gray, but the lines . . . the lines were lines. They were sharp and clear; you could see both hemispheres, and the ventricles ran true throughout. It was symmetrical, that normal brain, and it was beautiful in its symmetry.

The doctor stood looking, and he didn't nod. I didn't nod either. I stared at the lines in that stranger's brain, so clear and sharp, so unlike the lines in my sister's brain.

"Can you see, Miss Latham? There's a huge amount of bruised brain in your sister's head."

They drilled a little hole in her skull to suck out a blood clot and to take out her cerebrospinal fluid. They kept her calm. They kept track of the electrolytes in her blood.

"And that's about it. It's primitive, Miss Latham, but it's about all that we can do."

Then they did the tests, and Ivy was a no, a no, a no, a no, and another no—and then she tried to take a breath.

"So she's not brain-dead," my mother said to the doctor. "She tried to take a breath, so she's not brain-dead."

The doctor closed his eyes.

"She's not brain-dead," my mother said. "Right?"

"Not officially," he said. "Not legally."

Now the blood flows in her body because they keep her breathing with the ventilator. They feed her through a tube in her stomach. My sister who used to be moving water is now still water.

Route 365 north out of Sterns leads to Hinckley Reservoir, which before it was a lake was a town, the town of Hinckley. People used to live there, in houses, in trailers. There was a school and a post office and probably a store or two. No one remembers for sure.

The town of Hinckley flooded when they put the dam in. I think about that sometimes. I think of everything that happened in those homes, all the thousands of moments that make up the lives of the people who live there. Then the water came. The water came and washed away the fingerprints and footprints that marked all the places where people had ever been, had ever touched, had ever laughed and lived.

Hinckley is our own Pompeii, I say silently to Ivy as I walk.

Hinckley is nothing like Pompeii, I imagine her saying back to me. *Those Hinckley-ites had plenty of time to get out. I have no sympathy for anyone who drowned in the Hinckley flooding, if anyone even did drown in the Hinckley flooding. So there.*

That's what I imagine Ivy would say. If she could say anything. If she could think anything. If she could hear anything.

Hinckley is your *Pompeii, Rosie. Yours, not mine.*

Hinckley Reservoir is a placid surface. You'd never know that you were swimming on the graveyard of a town. All those houses, all those sidewalks, that school even, way down below. Goodbye, town. Goodbye, footprints, and goodbye, fingerprints.

Walk.

Keep walking.

For God's sake, Rose, do you want to be late for science? Or history? No. Certainly not. God forbid I should be late for history, and the book of wars, and the vast wisdom contained therein. *Rose, are you being sarcastic? No, Rose, I'm not being sarcastic.* Everyone needs to know everything possible about war.

Sometimes I hold conversations between myself and myself.

But at the intersection of Crill Road and Thompson Road, halfway to school, I stop: Help. I've walked for miles and the waters are not quieted. Will they overflow this time? Where's Todd? Where's Warren? Where's Jimmy Wilson with his rigid not-moving eyes that won't look at me anymore?

Ivy and I had an accident. It was dusk in the Adirondacks, and a light blue truck came around the curve—

"Younger." It's William T. He's rapping on the side of his truck, idling next to me. How long has he been there?

"Younger! Snap out of it!"

There's a look on his face.

"Hop in."

My feet won't move. I'm stuck.

"Now."

I get in. He drives me the rest of the way, into the high

school drop-off semicircle, and sits there with the truck still idling.

"Listen to me," he says. "Get out of the truck. Point your feet toward those doors and walk on in. Walk to your class. Walk to your next class. And walk to the class after that one."

That look on his face.

"Fifteen minutes at a time," he says. "Fifteen minutes. That's all you've got to think about."

But I'm tired. So tired. William T. leans across me and opens up the door and gives me a little push with the heel of his hand.

"Onward," he says. "I'll be back at three. That's twenty-seven fifteen-minute blocks from now."

I watch William T.'s truck disappear down the hill. Fifteen minutes. Then there I am, standing up at the front of the class holding my late pass.

Everyone's staring.

I hold it in, hold it all in. Fifteen minutes. I can feel all the eyes, glancing at me and trying to glance away, the eyes that see I'm not looking at them and therefore it's safe, safe to look at me, to take me in—what I'm wearing, how my hair is brushed or not, the way I stand up there at the desk waiting, waiting, waiting, waiting, waiting for Mr. Trehorn to take my late pass so that I can walk on back to the back.

Where Tom Miller waits.

Look up, Mr. Trehorn. Look up, Mr. Trehorn. Take the pass. Take the pass, Mr. Trehorn.

He's a busy man, Mr. Trehorn. He's extremely busy, making small black marks in his grade book. Mark, mark, mark. Busy, busy, busy.

Tom Miller gets up. He walks up to the front, where Mr. Trehorn's head is bent over his small black marks. Tom takes the slip of paper from my hand. Drops it on the desk.

"Knock, knock," he says to the bent head of Mr. Trehorn.

He waits for me to go first. I go first. Down the row I go. All the eyes. The eyes. The eyes. I can feel them. Rose Latham, whose sister was in the accident. Fifteen minutes. Tom Miller follows behind me. Fifteen minutes.

Now there are only two wars left: Vietnam and the Persian Gulf. Tracy Benova had tried to fill me in on what I had missed.

"World War II got the most attention," she said. "Korea was more of a blip. Korea seems to be the war when they stopped being so proud of wars."

I sit next to Tom Miller in the back of Mr. Trehorn's classroom. I didn't used to be a back-of-the-classroom student. But it's not so bad, being in the back, the backs of everyone's heads spread out before me, Mr. Trehorn standing up at the board, turning to write something down, turning back to explain what he's written down. Notebooks open. Pens scratching. Legs stretched in the aisle. The windows open and the sound of the birds outside, and the custodian mowing the far edge of the school grounds, next to the trees that line the edge of the soccer field.

Once in a while someone's head swivels to the back, to sneak a peek at me. Rose Latham with the brain-dead sister. Rose Latham who used to sit in the front row. Rose Latham the slut. Next to me Tom Miller doodles in his notebook.

Warren Graves turns around and looks at me. I meet his gaze. *Think you can hurt me, Warren? You have no idea.* Warren turns back around.

"Tet," Mr. Trehorn says. "Mekong. My Lai. Are these terms familiar to you?"

Heads nod.

"Why? Tell me what you know."

Hands raise. Mr. Trehorn stands at the board rolling the marker between his palms. A clicking sound each time it strikes his wedding ring.

"My grandfather said we could have won it, but they didn't let us win it."

"My uncle from Cleveland was a conscientious objector, and they put him in jail for two years."

"My mother worked at the base then; that was before

she quit. But she says she still remembers the planes flying out, all night long some nights."

Assignment. Copy it down.

What was the main reason the United States military decided to become a presence in Vietnam?

What was the military history of the United States in Southeast Asia that preceded the Vietnam War?

Why did the Tet Offensive come as such a shock?

Joe Miller once told Ivy that Tom Miller's father, Chase, hadn't wanted to go to Vietnam. That his draft number was called but that he wanted to go to Canada instead. But Spooner was all for the war. Spooner used to work at Griffiss Air Base even. Spooner was ashamed of his son. Wanting to avoid his patriotic duty.

Next to me Tom Miller is silent. Doodling away.

Fifteen minutes.

The un-bell unleashes itself from the loudspeaker.

My locker, still broken. I didn't get a new lock for it. Why bother? Nothing of value in it, unless you count outgrown sneakers and crumpled doodled-on notebook paper. A sweatshirt still hanging in there from before Ivy and I had the accident, when it was still winter, still cold. And the broken-spined book of wars.

The buses leave one after another, grinding out of the driveway, blue exhaust fading into the blue May sky, heading down Thompson Road into Sterns, or up Thompson Road into the foothills. Where's William T.? I've waited my twenty-seven fifteen-minute blocks, counted each one out, and he promised that after twenty-seven of them he would be here to pick me up. Down on the curb I sit and bend over my backpack, filled with the books I don't want to read.

"Rose."

Tom Miller's voice. I nod into my backpack. *I'm here, Tom Miller, and I hear you,* but it's too much effort to think of opening my eyes or lifting my head. I made it through all those fifteen minutes and now I'm tired. So tired.

"You waiting for William T.?"

I nod into my backpack again.

"He taking you down to see Ivy?"

Nod.

"Isn't he supposed to be here by now? William T.'s never late."

Nod.

"Rose. Lift your head up from that goddamned backpack and talk to me."

Shake.

His palm presses the back of my neck, a warm solid weight.

"You want me to take you down to Utica instead?"

Shake.

"You don't have to stay with me," I say. "William T.'ll be here."

"I know he'll be here. I'm just offering to take you down now, is all."

He strokes my hair.

"I could take you," he says. "I haven't seen her since the night it happened, you know."

I squinch my eyes tighter shut in the darkness of the backpack.

"Neither has Joe," I say.

I didn't know I was going to say that. My voice keeps coming out and saying things on its own. Tom's hand keeps stroking my hair. The May sun beats down. It's dark with my eyes shut tight and my face buried in my backpack and my arms imprisoning my knees.

"Not once," I say. "Not even one single time has Joe Miller been to see Ivy."

"I know," Tom says. "I know he hasn't."

"First my mother, and now Joe," I say. "What the hell is wrong with them? Don't they care about her? Don't they *love* her?"

More things I didn't know I was going to say. Tom's hand keeps stroking.

"It's tearing Joe up," he said. "He can't talk about it."

William T.'s pickup is coming down Thompson

Road. His pickup has an unmistakable this-is-William-T.'s-pickup sound. Half a mile away it can be heard. I keep my head in my backpack. Tom's hand disappears.

"Younger!"

The engine dies and William T.'s door opens with its William-T.'s-truck-door sound. He and Tom talk over my head.

"She all right?"

"She's okay."

I feel William T. kneeling next to me. His hand on my shoulder, so different from Tom's palm on my hair.

"Younger," he says. "Younger."

Open your eyes, Rose. Lift your head from the backpack. Ouch. The May sky is too bright. The little new leaves on the trees are too green. William T.'s eyes are bright and swimmy. Tears.

"I'm sorry I'm late, Younger. The truck's out of oil and I stopped at Agway to buy a quart but they were closed and then I saw I was late so I came on down anyway and here I am. Late. And the goddamned engine's about to seize up for all I know."

Tears slide out of his eyes down his rough cheeks.

"Gray's is open," Tom says. "Should be, anyway."

William T.'s hand on my shoulder is heavy.

"You want to head down to Utica, Younger? We could stop at Gray's first. But we don't have to. Go to Utica, that is. Not if you're not up to it."

If we don't head down to Utica, who will visit Ivy? I look at William T.

"Angel can take care of her for an afternoon," he whispers. He can read my thoughts. "Elder'll be all right until tomorrow."

I'm tired. So tired. But no. Ivy is waiting. We are already late. *I'm sorry, Ivy. Sorry for being late. William T.'s truck is out of oil.*

"Let's go," I say.

"Okay," William T. says. "To Utica we go, then, with a stop at Gray's for an oil change first. The truck's nine thousand miles overdue."

William T. nods at Tom, and Tom starts walking backward in the direction of the school parking lot. He flips his hand up in a wave to William T. and then turns around and jogs away. Into William T.'s truck I climb. Tired. Straight past my house we drive, and straight up William T.'s hill, and then a left onto Fuller Road, and all the way to Remsen we don't say a word. Once in a while William T. reaches over and puts his hand on my shoulder, then takes it off to steer around a curve. Lots of curves, here in the Adirondacks.

Joe Miller stands behind the counter at Gray's, sorting through scrawled-on pieces of paper all stamped Gray's Automotive, Remsen, New York.

"I used to change the goddamned oil myself, Joe," William T. says. "Now I say the hell with it."

He fishes a quarter out of his pocket and slaps it into my hand.

"Now I let you Millers do it for me. Splurge in my old age."

Into the restroom he goes. Joe stands behind the counter, sorting. One spike for the white scraps of paper, one spike for the yellow, the trash basket for the rest. His hair hangs down to his shoulders, and he swipes it back with a greasy hand. Dark hair, wavy. Not sun-streaked yet, the way it gets when the summer sun beats down upon his head.

Would I give up my hair, to get my sister back? Of course. My skull would tan in the summer and be egg-white in the winter. I would wear hats three seasons out of the year. I would give up all my hair. No hair anywhere. Eyebrows, eyelashes, all gone.

A sacrifice, but enough of one?

Of course not.

Joe's fingers are busy. He's almost through with one big stack. Soon he will be on to the next.

"What would you give up to have Ivy back the way she was?" I say.

He looks at me with a who-the-hell-do-you-think-I-am look. He shakes his head, and he goes back to his sorting.

"Nothing?"

"Stop it."

"If it were possible, I mean. If you could."

Sort. Spike. Toss. Sort. Sort. Spike. Toss.

"It's not possible," he says.

"But if it were. Imagine if it were. What would you be willing to give up?"

"Jesus Christ, Rose. Anything."

That's his answer. Anything. He doesn't stop to think. He doesn't go through the machinations, as William T. would have said, the machinations of analysis. The endless process. The series of what-if's and but-if's, the if-this-then-not-that's.

"So you would give up anything, then?"

His fingers stop flickering through the scraps of paper. He leans over the counter toward me.

"There is nothing I would not give up."

CHAPTER SIX

"You can't walk everywhere for the rest of your life, Younger," William T. says. "There are times when a car is a necessity."

He sits in his blue chair. I'm in my green chair with the chrome handles, one hand on Ivy's leg through the white sheet and the white blanket.

"The Pompeians didn't have cars," I say.

"My point exactly. Had the Pompeians had cars, they could've gotten the hell out of Dodge, so to speak. Outstripped that lava. Made it to an olive grove, taken shelter in the shade."

"I don't want to drive, William T."

"I know you don't, Younger. Nevertheless."

He holds out a New York State Department of Motor Vehicles driver's manual.

"Study up on the rules of the road," he says. "So that someday, if you decide that you might after all give it a try, you'll be prepared."

The car that Ivy and I were in was a station wagon. Now it's a lump of crushed metal that used to be a station wagon. In my imagination, our crushed car was perfectly square, the kind of square that appears in third-grade math books. One inch on every side. What is the perimeter of this square?

If you were me as a third grader, you did what the teacher told you to do and counted all the sides:

$$1 + 1 + 1 + 1 = 4$$

If you were Ivy as a third grader, you took one look and said, "Four."

Ivy didn't bother with the process. The process was what the math books wanted you to bother with, but Ivy didn't care. Instead of learning multiplication the way the book wanted you to—which was to understand the concept, and they had all kinds of ways to help you understand the concept—Ivy just sat down and memorized the times table. She made herself flash cards, the ones table through the twelves table, and sat there for a week. Every afternoon after school, every morning after breakfast, every night after dinner, until she had them down. Done.

I open the manual at random.

If you want to make a left turn from a one-way road onto a two-way road, you must approach the turn in the left lane or from the left side of a single lane. As you cross the intersection, enter the two-way road to the right of its center line, but as close as possible to the center line. Be alert for traffic, especially motorcycles, approaching from the road to the left. Oncoming motorcycles are difficult to see, and it is difficult to judge their speed and distance away.

"Read aloud," William T. says. "Maybe I'll learn something."

"'Single broken line,'" I read. "'You may pass other vehicles or change lanes if you can do so safely and not interfere with traffic.'"

"Well, hell, who doesn't know that one?"

"'If two drivers enter an intersection from opposite directions at the same time, one going straight, the other turning left, which must yield the right of way?'"

"Jesus. Ask me something I don't know."

"'What's the hand signal for right turn?'"

William T. frowns. He raises his left hand straight up

in the air and studies it, then drops it by his side, then holds it straight out.

"Goddamn. I think you've got me, Younger."

"Didn't take much. Quarter, please."

"What's the answer?"

I wave the manual at him. "Study up on the rules of the road. You might learn something."

William T. laughs. "You're a tough customer, Younger."

"'Solid line with broken line,'" I read. "'If you're on the side with the solid line, you may not pass other vehicles or cross the line except to make a left turn into a driveway. If you're on the side with the broken line, you may pass if it is safe to do so and your driving will not interfere with traffic.'"

"Duh," William T. says.

"'Single solid line,'" I read. "'You may pass other vehicles or change lanes, but you should do so only if obstructions in the road make it necessary or traffic conditions require it. With regard to a left turn from a one-way road onto another one-way road, prepare to turn by getting into the left lane, or the left side of a single lane, as close as possible to the left curb or edge of the road. If the road you enter has two lanes, you must turn into its left lane.'"

"Jesus, there's a lot of rules in that thing," William T. says.

"You should know. You must have studied it when you were getting your license."

"If I did, I have no memory of it."

I look at Ivy, sister with hands folded in front of her heart as if she is keeping them warm, as if she is praying, as if she is pleading, as if she is holding her own self together. Ivy and I had an accident. It was dusk in the Adirondacks that night, and we were coming around a curve.

"I don't want to drive," I say.

"To live in this world you must drive," William T. says.

"I'll live in another world, then."

I shut the driver's manual and pick up my Pompeii book again.

"Imagine it," I pretend-read. "All those ordinary people, living their ordinary lives. Maybe the baby had just gone to sleep in his basket of rushes in the corner."

"Basket of rushes?" William T. says. "I thought that was Moses."

"The baby is asleep in his basket of rushes," I pretend-read. "And his mother stands at the clay oven baking the bread for lunch, and his father is at the marketplace selling flagons of homemade wine."

"How is it possible that Moses was a Pompeian and all this time I never knew?" William T. says.

The door handle turns, and we both look up, ready to

greet Angel. But it's not Angel. It's Tom Miller and Joe Miller. Joe looks like an animal who has never been indoors before. "It's a crime, to keep a Miller confined," William T. said once.

Joe Miller stands there with his Gray's Automotive cap in his hands. There he stands, Tom behind him. It is the end of May, and Ivy has been on the ventilator for over two months. I watch Joe behold her, my sister Ivy with the tube in her throat and the tube in her arm and the tubes you can't see, underneath the sheet. Joe Miller turns and turns and turns his cap.

"Ivy?"

That's Joe, his voice. Low. Quiet. Saying her name. Can she hear him? Is she there? Joe watches Ivy, and I watch Joe, and Tom watches Joe, and Ivy with her closed eyes watches nothing.

"Ivy?"

Joe puts his cap on the table. He kneels by Ivy's bed.

"Ivy."

He says her name, and again he says her name.

"Ivy."

He reaches his hands to Ivy's, to Ivy's hands that lie cradled one inside the other. He folds his fingers around hers.

"Ivy," Joe whispers.

Then his eyes close. He brings my sister's folded hands to his cheek and rubs his cheek along the bundle of hands, four hands, that are his hands encircling my sister's hands. He rubs his face against my sister's hands, and he whispers her name, and I close my eyes and listen to him: "Ivy, Ivy, Ivy."

Ivy, when your head hit the steering wheel, did you know that I was next to you? I saw your face just before the light blue truck finished its slide—its slide that looked so gentle—and met our car. You looked blank.

Joe Miller turns away from the bed and walks to the door. Tom starts up from the floor where he sits, but Joe flicks his hand and Tom sinks back down.

"She would have hated this," Joe says to me. "She would've fucking hated this."

He pushes at the door and it stays motionless. He jerks at the handle and it swings in at him. He shoves out the door. He's gone. Tom turns to me and William T., shrugs: *I'm sorry.* Then he, too, is gone, gone after his cousin, gone to take him home.

The still water of Hinckley Reservoir covers what used to be: an entire town, the structure and framework of a thousand people's lives.

Does water have a memory? Does water remember where it came from, what it used to be? Does a drop of rain that falls in the middle of the opening bud remember that it used to be a frozen crystal under someone's gliding skate?

"I can't lose my girl," my mother said to the doctors.

She stood in the hall of the hospital, surrounded by them—the nurses, the doctors, the white coats and the blue scrubs, and the light flashing off eyeglasses and pens. Hands held at their sides, hands clutching papers or instruments, hands jammed in pockets.

My mother put her hands over her ears.

"I can't lose my girl."

She closed her eyes.

"I can't lose my girl. Can't lose my girl. Can't lose my girl."

Words rose around my mother, whose eyes were closed and whose hands were over her ears. What were the words? I don't remember. It doesn't matter.

Let her go is what they were saying.

They didn't use those words. They never would. They take a vow called the Hippocratic oath. It must go against everything in their training, to think of letting someone just . . . die. Just stop.

Stop breathing. Stop beating. Stop being.

Let her go.

I can't lose my daughter.

Let her go.

I can't lose my daughter.

I stood against the wall down the hall and watched. It went on for some time. The circle of men and women stood around my mother. The gentle wash of their voices continued. My mother was the lone center, her eyes closed and her hands over her ears, her face squinched shut, turning and turning and turning in a circle.

Ivy, are you somewhere else now? Does your spirit hover over that patch of road?

My sister and I had an accident. It was dusk in the Adirondacks that night. A boy who had just gotten his license came slipping and sliding down the mountains not knowing that he should be going slower, that it was a long curve, that it was icy here and there, and his light blue pickup truck didn't stop when he put on his brakes, and it slid into our car that Ivy was driving.

It happened so gently. I was with Ivy, sitting beside her. And I was looking through the windshield, at the diamond-light sky, and I saw the truck coming and I knew that it wouldn't be able to stop. It was going to happen. The truck would slide, and it would be soundless, and it would turn sideways toward us, and then it would turn again so that its front would be pointed directly at the car. It's happening again—

On the way home from Ivy's room, William T. stops at the Utica A&P. He wants to buy his girlfriend, Crystal, some green olives stuffed with garlic, which Crystal likes and which they don't sell at Jewell's Grocery. William T. loves to make Crystal happy.

"Garlic-stuffed olives for Crystal!" he says through

the window to me. He holds up his right hand and blinks his fingers three times. "Fifteen minutes. Sit tight, Younger. Fifteen minutes."

In the truck I sit, waiting for him. An old lady comes out of the A&P carrying a brown paper bag of groceries. She's an old lady, old old. Her days of walking well, of not thinking about walking, are long behind her. Now her every step is fraught. Her every step is something she thinks about, even now, in May, when winter is a memory.

Is that a puddle?

Is that a curb?

Mustn't fall. Mustn't fall. Mustn't fall.

Are those the thoughts of the old lady? Is that her mantra? I look at her and imagine that she's only trying to get back across the street into the Olbiston apartment building. Maybe she has a cat, a cat lying in a blue velvet chair, waiting for the old lady who has to think about Every, Single, Step.

But she doesn't fall. She makes her way slowly and steadily across the street. I cheer her on from my seat in William T.'s truck.

Then the bag splits. The old lady's cans and boxes roll around on the sidewalk, off the curb, into a puddle.

I shove open William T.'s truck door and run. *Quick, Rose, pick up all the groceries and set them beside the old lady.* She stands there trembling.

"Wait! I'll be right back!"

I hold my hand up. "Two minutes! Wait!"

Then I run into the A&P and grab a couple of plastic bags from the cashier and run back out. She's still standing there. Trembling. I crouch at her feet. She's wearing stockings. Old ladies always wear stockings. She's wearing old lady black rubber boots with fur at the top even though it's May, and gloves, and a hat, and an old lady black coat because old ladies are always cold.

I put all the groceries—the cans and boxes and bottles, the lamb chop and the two long carrots and the one onion and the head of lettuce—into the plastic bag. Then I put that bag inside the other bag.

"There you go."

"Thank you."

She doesn't look at me. She's too far gone into what just happened.

"Can I help you across the street?"

"Thank you."

But she can barely move. Her mouth is trembling. Her eyes are moving around, casting about on the sidewalk.

"Let me help you."

But I can't. That's the worst thing. I can't really help the old lady. I can run around and pick up all her groceries and put them in a plastic bag and take her arm and guide her across the street and raise my fist at a car that's going too fast and splashes us both with dirty brown water. I can walk her slowly, slowly, slowly, up the ramp into the brick building. I can hold the door for her, breathe in the stuffy indoor old-apartment-cooking-food-knocking-radiator smell of the building. But I can't help her the way I want to help her. I can't bring her back her legs. I can't bring her back her youth. I can't bring her back to a time in her life when someone stood beside her laughing and holding her hand.

"Thank you," she says.

"Anytime!" I say in a cheerleader voice. "No problem!"

William T. waits in the truck, watching me cross the street from the old lady's apartment building.

"What was that about?" he says.

I shake my head. Inside me I'm all exclamation marks, small streaks of lightning stabbing.

"She all right?" William T. says, looking across the street to where the old lady disappeared into the building.

I shake my head.

"Are you all right?"

I shake my head.

William T. puts the truck in gear and pulls out of the A&P parking lot. He points us north, to where the foothills are rising up, and eases into traffic.

"Home?" he asks after a while. After about fifteen minutes. Another fifteen minutes, and we will be at my driveway.

I shake my head.

"You want to go to skip stones at the Sterns Gorge, then?" he says. "We could have a contest, like we used to way back when."

"No!"

I can feel him looking at me. *Stop looking at me, William T.*

"That was a pretty big no," he says after a while. "Any particular reason for that?"

"No!"

"Younger."

"No! No! No!"

Exclamation points, jabbing and stabbing inside me. I sit in the truck and rock. Rock. Rock. Try to rock the water inside me, loosen it from its still lakes and overflowing oceans. There is not enough room in my body to contain all the water overflowing its banks. Will there ever be?

CHAPTER SEVEN

Hello June.

Goodbye March, when it happened, and goodbye April, when Ivy slept, and goodbye May, when Ivy slept, and hello June, and Ivy sleeps on.

"'Be prepared and look ahead,'" I read from the manual. "'You should sit comfortably, but upright, and keep both hands on the steering wheel. Slumping in the driver's seat or steering with one hand makes it harder to control your vehicle, and your "relaxed" position can lead to a dangerously relaxed attitude toward driving.'"

Could you stop reading that damn thing? Ivy doesn't say.

"'Anticipate mistakes by other drivers and think about what you will do if a mistake does happen. For example, do not always assume that a driver approaching a STOP or YIELD sign on a side road is actually going to stop or yield. It is better to assume the other driver may not stop. Be ready to react.'"

Give it a rest, Rose! Ivy doesn't say.

"To live in this world, Ivy," I pretend-read from the book, "you must know how to drive."

This world of roads and highways and cars and trucks and stop signs and blinking red lights and yellow lights that mean caution and green lights that mean go and engines that can throw a rod and tires that can go flat and brakes that can fail and air bags that may not inflate and gas stations, the endless ugliness of gas stations with their hoses and their pumps and their stink of gasoline.

To live in this world, you didn't always have to know how to drive. Once upon a time, people rode horseback. Once upon a time, the inhabitants of this world walked on foot, carrying their belongings in packs. Once upon a time the inhabitants of Pompeii ran, carrying their children in their arms.

I close the manual. Let Ivy sleep. *Sleep, sister, sleep.*

"You ever have a dream where you're falling, Younger?" William T. says from the blue chair. "One of those falling dreams? Jesus Christ, I hate those falling dreams."

"Sometimes," I say. "What brought on that comment?"

"Nothing in particular."

I turn around in my green chair and look at him, bent over the little table, pencil clutched in his big hand, underlining sentences in his bird book. I open the driver's manual again.

"'Sometimes it's better not to make eye contact with another driver, especially where conflict can occur,'" I read to William T. "'The other driver may interpret eye contact as a "challenge."'"

"That's true," William T. says. "God knows I've run into enough of that up on Route 12."

"'If confronted by an aggressive driver, stay calm and relaxed. Make every attempt to get out of the way safely. Do not escalate the situation.'"

"Never escalate," William T. says. "And never de-escalate, as in a falling dream. Excellent advice."

"'Put your pride in the back seat. Do not challenge an aggressive driver by speeding up or attempting to hold your position in your travel lane.'"

"Especially if he's a Statie," William T. says. "Those troopers take their travel lane position very seriously."

"'No matter how carefully you drive, there is always a chance that you will be involved in a traffic crash. You cannot predict when it may happen.'"

William T. is silent. He bends over his bird book.

"William T.," I say, "when your son died, what did you do?"

His pencil hovers a fraction of an inch over the page. Searching, searching. For what? He doesn't look up.

"I wanted to die too," he says.

His pencil keeps hovering. Then I watch it underline a sentence swiftly and surely. Then another one. Another one. The pencil is a speed skater, practicing for the Olympics.

"But I kept on living," William T. says. "It's a weird thing, Younger, how sometimes we think we can't, but we do. We just keep on living."

Ivy and I had an accident. It was dusk in the Adirondacks that night. Ivy's foot pumped the brake when the light blue truck began to slide toward us. She knew what to do and she did it. She pumped lightly and quickly, her foot in its black winter boot moving like a piston on the brake. The boy in the light blue truck was wearing brown work boots. He was from Remsen. It was only his third time alone in the truck. That's what his mother told me.

"Had I known what would happen," she said, "I never would have let him go."

DUH, I thought. It's weird how sometimes part of your mind can be separate from the rest of you, and think things like *DUH*.

"Younger?"

"William T.?"

"How's your driving coming along?"

"It's not."

"Well, it better. I got you an appointment for a road test."

"You what?"

"You heard me."

"William T., I can't take my road test yet. I don't know how to drive!"

"Learn, then. Because the appointment is three short weeks away. Get on it, Younger. Hop to it like the bird of the day—a greater yellowlegs sandpiper—would hop to it, trim and alert and dashing about in shallow waters."

I roll my eyes.

"What?" William T. says. "You got something against sandpipers?"

I turn back to the manual.

"'Chapter Eight: Defensive Driving,'" I read to Ivy.

"Always drive defensively," William T. agrees. "That is rule number one. Drive as if the other person is crazy. Or drunk. Expect the unexpected."

"What are you, the peanut gallery? I'm not reading this to you, William T. Go back to your sandpipers."

"I'm finished with sandpipers. On to pewees and tyrannulets, drab flycatchers that perch upright."

"'Almost all drivers consider themselves good drivers,'" I read aloud.

"But when you come right down to it, Younger, most of them are piss-poor drivers."

"'To avoid making mistakes yourself or being involved in a traffic crash because of someone else's mistake, learn to drive defensively.'"

"Didn't I tell you? Rule number one."

"No, you didn't tell me. The manual told me. 'The defensive driving rules are simple. Be prepared and look ahead. Maintain the proper speed. Signal before turning or changing lanes. Allow yourself space. Wear your seat belt. Do not drive if you are very tired, are on medication, or have been drinking alcoholic beverages. And finally, keep your vehicle in good operating condition.'"

"'Keep your vehicle in good operating condition,'" William T. repeats. "Excellent advice."

Excellent advice? William T.'s own truck is a mess. The passenger door doesn't open; the heat doesn't work; the horn mews; and even after you fill it up, the gas registers perpetually empty. I give him a look. He shrugs.

"Do as I say, not as I do, Younger. Who the hell's perfect? Not me."

Not me either.

"The hell with the driver's manual."

"Younger, did I just hear you curse?"

"No. I would never curse."

"Younger, are you being sarcastic with me?"

"No. I would never be sarcastic with you, William T. Nor would I be acerbic or mordant."

"*Mordant?* What the hell does *mordant* mean?"

"I'll tell you what *mordant* means if you tell me what the hell we're doing here, William T.," I say. "What the hell are we doing here with Ivy? In thirty years, will we still be here?"

"I hope so," William T. says. "I hope that thirty years hence, I will be sitting in the back seat of a car in good operating condition that my Younger will be driving defensively, and my Elder will be sitting up front next to her, and we're looking back on this time and shaking our heads that we survived it all. That's what I hope."

That's the kind of thing that, once in a while when you least expect it, William T. says.

"Driving is easy, Younger, and so is driving stick," William T. says. "All you have to do is think like a truck."

We're sitting in the truck in the parking lot of the Rosewood Convalescent Home. We've said goodbye to Ivy and Angel. William T. wants me to practice my driving. Now.

"It's not possible to think like a truck," I say. "Trucks don't think. Trucks are not sentient beings."

"*Sentient?* What the hell does that mean?"

"Look it up."

"You're a tough customer, Younger."

"Not when it comes to driving."

If trucks were sentient beings, they would want to move. That's what wheels are for. That's what a gas pedal is for, to urge it forward; that's what windows are for, to open on a summer day so that the summer wind can blow clean and wild through a truck moving fast and far.

"Think like a truck anyway," William T. says. "Think like a truck would think if a truck *could* think."

"How much wood would a woodchuck chuck if a woodchuck could chuck wood?" I chant.

"Don't change the subject. To live in this world you must know how to drive, Younger. Let me give you a lesson."

"No."

"Because I could, you know. I'm a damn fine teacher."

"No."

"I taught my son to drive," he says. "By the book, too. Hands at ten and two, seat belt fastened at all times."

William T. hardly ever mentions his son. I look at him, but he doesn't look back at me.

To live in this world you must know how to drive.

After dinner, spaghetti that I make for my mother and me, I walk out to the end of the driveway, where the Datsun is parked. The driver's manual lies open on the seat next to me.

What should you do if you hear a siren nearby but cannot see where the emergency vehicle is? How far before a turn must you signal? When preparing for a right turn, should you stay as close to the center of the lane as possible? Where should you position your vehicle when preparing to make a left turn from a two-way roadway onto a one-way roadway?

Every time I try to advance, the truck stalls on me. How can I blame it? The screech and whine of tortured metal are almost too much for me too. *Easy on the gas; let up slowly on the clutch—both actions simultaneously.*

William T. has drilled that mantra into me, but I still can't get it right. Every time my right foot starts to push gently on the gas pedal, my left foot comes up too fast on the clutch. And every time I actually get going and need to upshift, my right hand shoves the stick too fast, before the clutch is "fully engaged."

Not good.

None of it good.

After a while, the truck has jerked across the road right into the corn field itself. The hell with it. I sit in the truck, both of us beings—one sentient, one not—in the field of young corn, soft green leaves caressing each other in the breeze. If at first you don't succeed. My right hand clutches the top of the gearshift. If each finger clenches as tight as it can possibly clench, then that will be the focus of my concentration, and I can resist shoving up on the knob too soon, before the clutch is fully engaged. That is my plan.

Right?

Wrong.

Before the accident, my sister's hands were always in motion. Like birds flying. Words came more easily for her when her hands were moving. The phone would ring for Ivy, and she'd start talking, holding the phone like an ordinary person. Then she would shift the phone to the crook of her neck, between her jaw and her shoulder. When her hands were free to fly, she relaxed. She would wander from room to room talking, hands flying.

Think like a truck? Trucks don't think. Trucks move. Trucks slide. A light blue truck slid toward me and my sister.

A long time ago, in the haymow, Ivy and I were playing truth or dare with Joe and Tom. Ivy lost and Joe gave her a dare. Whatever it was, it wasn't enough for Ivy.

"You call that a dare?" she said to Joe. "I sneer at thee."

"Okay," Joe said. "Then go stand in the window."

She hesitated. Ivy hated heights. We all knew it, but would she admit to it? No. Beyond us the paneless window gave onto the hill where the blackberries grew. The paneless window was more like a door. It began at the floor of the barn. It had been open as long as I could remember, a sheer drop to the hill below, with its blackberry canes and their thorns, and the rocks that surround the springhouse. Nothing to break your fall.

"Go on now, then," Joe said. "Stand in the window for ten seconds. I'll time you."

"What are you, man or mouse?" Ivy said. "More."

"More?"

"More. Give me your best shot."

In the darkness, Ivy and Joe looked at each other. My sister Ivy with her one fear: heights. Afraid to climb higher than a six-bale-high fort, afraid to swing on the swings at school, afraid of stairs without railings, the bald top of Bald Mountain. Every time I think of that night, that night in the haymow, it seems darker. I watched Ivy the way you would watch a stranger in the darkness. She was no longer a person with outlines and boundaries. She was only a being, a being wary of heights.

"Swing on the rope swing, then," Joe said to Ivy.

That was something she'd never done. The rope swing, a thick braided rope hung from the highest rafter, was my delight. I loved it, its freedom, the swish of the air on my face, my closed eyes as I leaped from the tallest stack of hay bales and swung, and swung, and swung, a human pendulum, until the rope slowed and I dropped from it onto the pile of hay. I love height. Mountains. Tall buildings, the way they rise straight from the solid earth, laddering themselves skyward as if trying to touch heaven, whatever heaven might be.

"Grab on to the rope swing," Joe said, "and swing right on out that window. Let's see you do it."

Ivy was silent.

"Time's a-wasting," Joe said.

Ivy stood there, a presence in the darkness. Beyond the small circle of the four of us, the paneless window was a rectangle of indigo in which stars were beginning to appear.

"Afraid?"

I reached out in the darkness to find my sister. I knew how much she hated heights.

"Ivy, you don't have to," I said.

She turned to me in the darkness.

"Ivy," Joe said. "What would you do if you weren't afraid?"

That was years ago. That was before Joe and Ivy were boyfriend and girlfriend, but long after the time when my mother stayed in bed, the time when William T. started making scrambled eggs for us and checking on us, the time when we were still children.

I sit in the truck and gaze out the windshield with its shivery line where a rock flung up from the pavement hit it. Think like a truck. The corn field is silent. Patient. The paneless window glimmers in my mind. Joe Miller teases my sister about being afraid. The waters are rising within me and want out. Out. Out.

Out of the truck. Dusk has gathered over the Sterns Valley. I start walking up 274 toward Remsen, and Gray's Automotive, and Joe Miller, Joe Miller who loves my sister.

By the time I get to Gray's, it's closed, but I tap on the window until Joe looks up from stocking the candy counter and comes around and shoves open the door for me. Something I want to say to Joe Miller, although now that I'm here, I don't know what it is.

"She's not officially brain-dead," I say. "She still has a respiratory drive."

Joe says nothing. The last of the sun plays through the smeary windows, sinking fast.

"A slight one," I say.

They turned the ventilator off and waited.

Waited.

Waited.

Waited.

And then she tried to breathe.

My mother, my thin, nervous, finger-tapping mother, carried my sister inside her for nine months and then pushed her into the world. My mother who spends her days righting bottles, bringing order to disorder in a twelve-foot-square patch of the Utica Club Brewery. Who cried to the doctor that she could not lose her daughter.

"They should've let her die," he says.

Joe stands behind the counter, giving me that look. I had thought that walking to Gray's Automotive, five miles north, would calm the waters. But no.

Ivy and Joe were moving water, and they moved together, and their bodies flowed toward each other, and they didn't stop to think, they didn't stop themselves, they wanted to move and move together, and they did. And Ivy came home late on summer nights and lay in her bed and fell into her easy sleep, her soft breath rising and mingling with the soft summer air, and I in my bed on the other side of the room was not free, was not part of the world the way she was, the way she always was. She was the Sterns Gorge, rushing and tumbling, dark shallow water in a hurry, and I am Hinckley Reservoir, contained and still.

Once there was a night when I watched Joe Miller bend over Ivy's foot. It was another night in the hay barn, and Joe was teaching Ivy and me how to drink from a beer bottle like a guy. We were sixteen and seventeen.

"You don't want to drink like a girl," Joe said. "A girl tips her whole head up."

He demonstrated. So? What was wrong with tipping your whole head up?

"You want to drink like a guy," he said. "Watch."

He tipped the bottle up while his head stayed put. One tan hand tilted the bottle, and the beer flowed steadily into his mouth. I watched him swallow. I watched Ivy watch him swallow. That's the thing about Millers. You can't not watch them, watch their bodies, watch their muscles and bone as they move their way through the world.

"Try it."

He passed the bottle to me.

"No, you're still tipping your head. It's the bottle you want to tip, not your head. Let Ivy try."

I passed the bottle to Ivy.

"Good."

Ivy took another swig and smiled at him. Joe smiled back the way he smiles—only one side of his mouth goes up. I watched her watch him, and I watched him watch her back. He bent his head and then he picked up her foot. Her bare foot with the purple toenail polish she used to brush on. Every Sunday night: off with the old, on with the new. His fingers circled her foot and he held it in both his cupped hands, as if her tan bare foot with its chipped purple toenail polish were something beloved.

After the accident, Joe Miller went crazy. Crazier than the Miller boys go is where Joe went. I remember looking up from the green counter in the kitchen where I was making coffee for my mother and there was Joe, standing on the porch, looking in at me through the window in the door. It was early morning. It had been only three days. They had just done the tests.

He pushed open the door and came in and stood on the boot mat. Waiting. As if his body wanted to be on to its next movement but he must first wait for it to finish this one.

Joe looked at me. The kind of look a muskrat caught in a trap might have. Looking around at the trees and the grass and the creek, everywhere he wanted to be, and nowhere he could run to—and when he looked down for some relief from seeing all the places he couldn't go, all the places he had taken for granted, there was the steel trap on his leg. You could see why the muskrat would want to chew his leg off.

Joe Miller would chew his leg off.

"How is she?"

He was waiting in the way that he waits, which is all muscles tensed, all muscles ready to move. He looked at me across the kitchen and didn't blink. He waited. I stood there. For three days I had been sitting by my sister's bed. I had been holding her hand; I had been smoothing her hair back from her forehead, the part that wasn't covered with the bandage.

How is she?

Joe and Ivy had been together three years.

I shook my head. And then Joe Miller was gone, out the door and into his truck, body moving into the motion it longed for.

CHAPTER EIGHT

The bricks of Sterns High School are warm against my back. It's almost the end of the last day of school. Almost time to go home. Almost time for William T. to pick me up. Almost time to drive down to Ivy's room, where I will read to Ivy from the driver's manual. I pull my knees up and clasp my arms around them. And the scream rises within me, electricity prickling up and down my arms and legs, stabbing my heart with its tiny exclamation points. How did I get here? How did it happen that time picked my sister and me up last March, and stopped for a while, and then set me down again, here in June, just me, Rose alone?

To live in this world you must drive. But I don't drive.

Down at the Rosewood Convalescent Home, a ventilator pushes air into my sister's lungs: *wishhh, wishhh, wishhh.*

"They should've let her die," Joe Miller said. "They should've let her go."

Sometimes I can feel it all, all the hurt of the world balled up inside me. And when it comes over me like this, I am my mother hunched over her potholders; I am Joe Miller, who would do anything; I am Chase Miller, who never found his way home from Vietnam; I am William T., who lost his son; I am a tiny untouchable garden; I am a girl hovering over herself down on the rocks of the gorge with the boys; I am a ball of girl held tight, clenched, and the water is rising within, overflowing. Nowhere to go, nowhere to spill to, no river to tumble down, no ocean to disappear into—

A flutter of white drifts up into the sky. The fifth graders down the hill in Sterns Elementary are releasing their balloons. Balloons with notes inside them, bound for wherever they will end up, in hopes that someone, somewhere, will wake one morning a few weeks hence to see a balloon drifting downward. The balloon will come gradually to rest on the windowsill of that someone, that foreign someone who will release the tired old air from the tired old balloon. Rest, balloon, you must be worn out from your journey. *What have we here,* the foreign someone might think in her foreign language, *and who might it be from?*

Did the mother of the baby in his rush basket in Pompeii leave a note? Did she pause? Jot a few words in Latin for someone she loved to find later?

The white balloons tremble into the sky, higher and higher. At first they cluster together. Then the wind catches one, and then another, and off they go.

That night in the haymow, Joe Miller urged Ivy on.

"What are you, chicken? What are you, afraid?"

She jutted her chin out at him. This was years ago, when we were younger, when Ivy and Joe had yet to know what they came to know about each other, and about themselves together. Before I learned about the Higgs boson, and Pompeii, and the town of Hinckley, and dark matter. Outside the paneless window, the sky was nearly purple, a bruised plum. And the moon hung high and white.

"Don't be a jerk!" I said to Joe. "She could break her leg if she fell!"

"Ivy," Joe Miller said. "What would you do if you weren't afraid?"

And then she was running, and Joe was up and tossing the rope of the rope swing to her, and then she was swinging. She didn't have to, but she did. How different Joe Miller and I were. How different Ivy and I were. How different, how different, how unfair, how unfair.

"Happy summer, Rose. You made it."

Tom Miller stands before me, blocking the sun. I open my eyes. Unclasp my arms.

If I stood up and put my arms around him and kissed him, would he kiss me back? Would he meet me at the Sterns Gorge, shove himself against me? Is Tom Miller like Jimmy and Warren and Todd? His eyes narrow. There's a look on his face.

"What's going on with you?" he says.

"What do you mean?"

I hear my voice, sounding the way it sounds at the gorge, with the boys. Words coming out that I didn't plan on saying.

"Don't talk to me like that."

"Like what?"

"Like that."

I make my eyes big. We stand there like that. The un-bell screams from the speakers.

"SHUT UP!" I scream back.

"The bell?" Tom says. "Or me?"

The sound of the un-bell grinds inside me. Will I hear it for the rest of my life?

"The bell, you idiot!"

"Now I'm an idiot?"

"Yes. You're an idiot."

"Then I'm an idiot. But you're still not answering me. What's going on with you? What's up with Jimmy Wilson and Warren Graves?"

I shake my head. *Quiet, Tom Miller. Silence. No more.* He stands in front of me, blocking the sun. Yellow buses grind up the school driveway, crowding up one against the other on this, their last day of the school year. Their final journey until the fall. One after the other they nose up to the curb, rumble to a stop, engines dying with a long shuddering sigh.

"Are you trying to prove something?"

I shake my head.

"Then why?"

Shake. Still he stands in front of me. This afternoon, Warren and Todd stood huddled by Todd's locker. Something in the lines of their shoulders, their low voices. And Tom passed by them and stopped. Inclined his head toward them. And then he looked over at me and my broken combination lock, my locker, my hands clenching around my books.

The doors behind me open. Feet stampede past. Chatter and shrieks and cries and shouts spin off into the high blue sky above, invisible spirals of sound losing themselves past the green tops of the trees. Still Tom stands there. Voices call to him.

"Hey, Tom."

"Millerrrrrr."

"Miller!"

He says nothing. Then he's crouching on the ground in front of me.

"You going to talk to me?"

Shake. *No. I am not going to talk to you, Tom Miller.*

"Is William T. coming, then?"

"No."

"Why not?"

"Vet. For the flock."

"You want a ride home, then?"

Shake.

"Well, you better get on your bus, then, Rose-who-won't-talk. You wouldn't want to miss it."

The voices and shouts and chatter are quieter now, contained behind the closed windows of the buses, closed windows that are being opened now, one by one, shoved up with a rasping clatter. I nod. Okay. Better get on the bus, then. Last time. Last school bus day of the year.

This time it's not Warren or Todd or Jimmy—not Jimmy who still sits not looking at me, his head rigid every time I pass him in school. This time it's Kevin. Kevin who sits by me. Kevin who puts his arm around me.

"What's up, Rose?" Kevin says.

And the rigidity all around us. No one says anything. No one hoots. No one jeers. I stare out the window at the cornstalks. So green, the green of early summer, poor little cornstalks reaching to the sky.

"So," Kevin says. "You thinking of skipping rocks at the gorge today?"

Silence.

"Or tonight?"

Silence.

"I could meet you up there," Kevin whispers.

"No."

"No? Why not?"

"No."

"What's wrong with me? What, they got something I don't?"

"No."

"Come on, Rose. It'll be fun."

"NO." I shove him. Straight into the aisle. He sprawls there, his face open with surprise for half a second. In that half a second something flits over his face, a feeling. Hurt. *Why them and not me? What's wrong with me?* That's what he's thinking in that half second, and I think back at him, *It's not you; it's me.* But I can't say that. The half a second passes and he turns dark with anger. A flush of rage starts at his neck and floods upward, slitting his eyes. He jumps to his feet in the aisle. Everyone's watching.

"You're really fucked up, Rose. Did you know that?"

His fist clenches. He's holding back from hitting me.

"You're one fucked-up bitch," he says, and he turns around and walks up the aisle to where Todd sits and gazes back at me, the same slitted-eye look. And Warren. And Jimmy's head held rigid to the front.

Sound and movement ripple from the back to the front of the bus, washing over me. A green pickup pulls up alongside the bus. The green pickup's dulled by winters of sand and salt and snow, and it pulls alongside the bus on Route 274 up here in the foothills, where Katie disgorges us one by one by two. Tom Miller, flush with my window, keeping pace with the big yellow bus.

"Hey!" Katie yells, her voice a familiar grunt. "Get back! It's a two-lane road, asshole!"

A hand in the window of the green truck waves, fingers tapping on the smeared glass of the driver's window. I look down from my perch, the green vinyl of my seat the same green as the truck, at Tom Miller's waving fingers. His mouth shapes silent words.

Rose?

He taps again. He drives with one hand and keeps even with my window. Katie's angry, her arm wheeling in the air: *Out of the way!*

Rose?

"Rose, it's Tom Miller," Tracy Benova says importantly. "Rose, it's Tom! He wants you!"

Then Tom's tapping fingers are gone. The smeared

glass of the window clears, the pane pushing itself down into the recesses of the pickup's green door. Now his fingers are real, long and strong, his brown hair falling into eyes that aren't brown or blue but are a dark green with flecks of yellow. His voice takes shape, words floating clear in the blue stillness of the sky. Everyone on the bus can hear him.

"Rose!"

Up front, Katie shakes her fist. Angry Katie. Kids shift from the other side of the bus to crowd into the ones on my side: drama on the school bus, not to be missed. A one-act play being acted out right there on Route 274. Their faces press against windows, where dust coats the glass in a light brown film.

"Rose!"

I duck and bend and move to the empty side of the bus to crouch out of sight behind Katie, who's cursing, her face red. Turn away from the sight of Tom Miller's reaching hand. The driver's manual says it's better not to make eye contact with another driver when conflict is possible. *Stay calm and relaxed. Make every attempt to get out of the way safely. Do not escalate the situation.* Why? Because an accident may happen at any time. I stare out the new window at the green of cornstalks waving in the June breeze. Across the aisle North Sterns kids point and jabber, laughing and waving at Tom Miller driving half in the ditch, his fingers trying to pull a summer sky into his truck. Up the aisle Jimmy and Warren and Kevin sit like stone, not saying a word.

Then the bus stops.

I can't stop crying.

A hand.

I can't breathe.

A hand pulls me down onto a seat. Tom Miller. He pulls me down. I'm sitting. Someone says something I can't understand. My ears are full. Tom half rises out of the seat.

"Fuck off," he says.

The bus is quiet, and then there's sound. Normal sound, bus sound, talking, whispering, arguing, high-pitched shrieking, murmuring. I sit for a long time and concentrate on taking a breath and letting it out, taking a breath and letting it out.

"Here we are," Tom says. "Get up now."

He follows me down the stairs.

"Asshole," Katie spits. "You shouldn't be on this bus."

"But I am," Tom says.

"Don't ever pull that shit with me again."

"I don't plan to."

Together we walk up my driveway. Into my house. It creaks the way a house does when it's empty of people. You can tell. The air of a house changes when there is even one person in it, one person locked away in an upstairs bedroom, for example, taking a nap. A house knows when someone is in it and changes accordingly, shapes itself to fit the spirit and mood and presence of the person within. But when a house is empty, then it's the house's turn. It holds all the emptiness and all the fullness of the years it has known. The footprints of all the people who have ever walked its rooms gather themselves. The air is expectant, waiting. Hushed. Hush. Listen to the house. What is it telling you?

"Why are you doing this?" Tom says again.

We stand in the kitchen of my empty house, him facing me, my backpack slung over one shoulder and heavy, heavy, heavy. Tom carries nothing.

"Why are you doing this?" he says again. "Answer me."

I shake my head.

A dark night, and the stars shine thickly in the heavens.

The storms are up and the screens are propped up with sticks. Night fog comes stealing into my room from all sides, cross-ventilated from the three open windows. Sometimes, before dawn on a summer morning, the clouds come down to earth and the mist that rises from the grass rises to meet it. Sometimes a tendril of white curls through the mesh of my screened window. A finger. A hand, cupped and beckoning to me: *Come out and play. Come out and play.*

I can't sleep. Propped on my elbows, staring out at the darkness, listening to the owls. Headlights make their silent way down William T. Jones's hill, and I watch them as they approach, hear the familiar whine of its engine. Tom Miller, driving past in Spooner's truck. I watch him from my bedroom window, and I rise in the darkness and put on my T-shirt and shorts.

The road to the village glimmers in the darkness, as if mixed in with the rock and gravel and tar that made it is something luminescent. Fireflies flicker in the air around me. The pines and maples and oaks that line the road are silent, sap stilled in their veins.

I walk. Behind me my mother sleeps. Our house is dark, a dark shape in the darkness. I walk through waves of warm air and waves of cold, an early summer night and a girl alone on the road.

In the village I stop at the stop sign and turn right. I know where Tom Miller is, where he must be. The gazebo stands white and silent in the village green.

Chase Miller. And Tom, his son, leaning against the stone.

I sit beside him. Crickets scrape wings across backs and fill the night with song. Bats fly overhead and somewhere in the darkness a barred owl calls. After a while Tom closes his eyes and leans into the stone. The stone is always cool. Even in the heat of the day, when the sun beats on it for hours, its warmth is a surface warmth.

"Tom?"

He looks at me.

"Does it give you comfort, to have that stone?"

He nods.

I wish I had a stone. The churning begins inside me and rises. Tom Miller leans against his father's stone and I can feel how it would feel if I too were leaning against that stone. Stone beneath me and Jimmy Wilson on top of me. Stone against my back. Stone, skipping across the dark water of the gorge.

"Rosie?"

Tom Miller has never called me Rosie before, not even when we were little kids, back when all our little kid names ended in "y": Rosie and Tommy and Ivy and Joey.

"Can I sit next to you?" I say, and then the tears come. And the stone is warm behind my back, and Tom Miller's arms are around me. Tom sits and I sit until the sounds become part of the night sky, until the images in my mind become part of the darkness of the mountains rising up, until my skin is one with the stone, until I stop crying. Tom's arms are around me and we lean against polished rock. Our breathing softens and slows until it reflects the stillness of the night air. Then we rise and walk across the grass made wet by dew, into the truck, and he pushes open the passenger door for me, and we drive back up into the foothills.

CHAPTER NINE

"Come with me tomorrow," I say.

My mother folds a square of newspaper into a smaller square, into quarters, bends and folds and creases and smoothes and pushes, gently, gently. Delicate plucks and pushes.

"In Japan they believe that if you make a thousand paper cranes, your wish will come true," she says.

Thirty miles south, a ventilator pushes air into my sister's lungs: *wishhh, wishhh, wishhh.*

"Come with me."

"Miracles have been known to happen."

She folds another square of newsprint. Will she make a crane out of anything? Before she went to the brewery in the morning, she'd made a little pile, and when William T. took me back home after making me scrambled eggs, it was a big pile.

"You should have let her go."

Had I known I was going to say that? My mother looks up at me with those eyes of hers.

"You don't know. Someday they might be able to fix her," she says. "You don't know. Nobody knows."

"Someday? What about today?"

I spit the words. So angry. So angry. All I can think, all I can feel, is anger surging hot and strong like strong black coffee, strong and black through my veins and arteries, pulsing in and out of my heart.

"You don't know! It's *you* who doesn't know!"

My mother looks at me.

"You have not once been to see her! You are the one who doesn't know! You know nothing!"

My mother shakes her head.

"She would've hated this!" I scream. "She would've fucking hated this!"

"I hate this!" my mother screams back. "I hate this! I hate this!"

"I hate *you*!" I scream.

She keeps shaking her head. Her hands run over the surface of her paper cranes, quivering as if they were one animate creature, a trapped being, seeking refuge from the light of the lamp. I am still water. I am water trapped inside the cage of my body. I am water that wants out, that wants escape, that cannot stand the pressure of its own self, pulsing inside me.

She shakes and shakes and shakes her head.

If you want to live in this world, there is no way not to drive.

That's what William T. says.

The red Datsun is parked in the corn field. After a while of trying to move forward, then trying to move backward, and listening to the shrieks and groans of tortured metal, I turn the engine off and roll down my window and the passenger window too. Soft summer air blows through the open windows, and the sound of crickets rises about me. Under the hood, the engine ticks.

I sit in the corn field a long time.

Do I want to live in this world?

"Rose?"

Tom's voice. William T. Jones's hill is a big hill, half a mile long, and steep. If you're trying to drive up it in winter, do not stop. That's what I've heard the boys on the bus say. I didn't hear Tom driving down. Didn't hear him drive into the corn field, turn off Spooner's truck, open the rusted door, and climb out.

"Rose?"

His voice, coming through the open window.

"Rose."

His voice is no longer a question. A question has become a statement. I look up. His face, his Tom Miller face, peers in my window. He bends down outside the truck. His hair is sun-streaked already, brown turned dark blond by the long June days.

He taps on the window frame with his fingers. Tap tap.

"Stuck?"

I nod. Yes. I am stuck. Young cornstalks wave around us, green and leafy in the late afternoon sun. If I get out of the truck, the ground underneath them will be spongy. It will give beneath my feet, which are bare, the better to feel the pedals with. The better the feel, the easier the shift. That's been my philosophy, but my philosophy hasn't been working.

"Are you in neutral?" Tom asks.

He reaches in through the window and puts his hand on the gearshift. Wiggles it.

"Neutral," he says. "Turn it on."

I turn the key in the ignition and the truck starts up again with a quiet, patient sound. Maybe it doesn't mind that I keep putting it through grinding-of-gears torture. Maybe it knows that I'm just trying to figure it all out.

Tom walks around the front of the truck and holds his hand up, as if his hand alone will be enough to remind the truck that it's in neutral and can therefore slip forward, and that it shouldn't slip forward when a person is walking in front of it. The passenger door opens and then he's next to me.

"Okay, Rose."

He puts his hand over my fingers that are still wrapped around the knob of the gear stick.

"Come on."

He unpries my fingers, one at a time, from the knob. Then he drapes my hand back over the knob and wiggles each finger.

"You want your hands to be loose," he says. "Driving stick is one of those things. If you think about it too much, you can't do it. You have to go by instinct."

His hand over my hand is warm. Around us the young green leaves wave in the breeze and brush gently against each other, and cricket song rises into the twilight sky until it disappears.

"Easy in with the gas, and easy out with the clutch," Tom says.

The sun is beginning to set. Long shadows from the cornstalks lie over the hood of the truck. In little bits, I drive forward to the end of the field.

"Stop, slow."

And I stop, slowly.

"Go ahead, slow."

And I go slowly ahead.

It's a whole different ball game down at the end of the field. To back up, you have to push the gearshift all the way to the right and then up. The diagram on the knob doesn't do it justice.

"Don't look at that diagram, Rose. Go by feel instead."

He tells me to close my eyes.

"Go ahead," he says. "There's nothing to run into anyway, down here at the end of the corn field. Just close your eyes and feel where the stick needs to go."

I close my eyes. I push the stick around a little bit, up and down, back and forth. I listen to the long brushing leaves of green, cornstalk leaves, arching down upon the hood of the little red truck as we stutter along.

"Go ahead and test it out on the corn itself," Tom says. "Drive down a row."

I open my eyes. The rays of the setting sun filter through the corn, stretching ahead of us. We're at the end of the field, the woods behind us and the green waving stalks in front. The sun has sunk below the level of the highest leaves, and the air is bathed in soft pink and orange and blue, the colors of an ending day.

"Give it a try, Rose. Take a walk on the wild side."

Tom smiles at me. It's William T.'s corn. He grows it for the hell of it, he says, the sheer hell of it, because he likes the look of the tall waves of green. I know that he grows it for more than that, though. He feeds it to his flock, his flock of lame birds, the chickens and the geese and the ducks that he keeps in his broken-down barn.

"It's just cow corn. Mow it down. Why are you restraining yourself?"

The just-cow-corn stretches itself in front of me, rippling in the breeze that sometimes springs up just before sunset, when the world quiets itself for the passing of the light. It's just cow corn, but it's William T.'s cow corn.

"Go on," Tom says.

"No. I don't want to."

He looks at me. I look at him, too, but only for a second. When William T.'s son was still alive he—William T.'s son—would sometimes drive past our house in his truck, and he would stick his hand out the window if we were on the lawn, and he would wave and call to us. Sometimes he would be singing. William T.'s son loved to sing, and he would wave and keep right on singing, not say hi, just sing, and his truck would go around the bend and then the song would be gone.

"No?" Tom says.

A seed is dropped on the fertile earth, and the sun shines on it and the rain rains down, and days pass and nights, too, and a stalk of corn grows and grows and grows into the world, giving to and receiving from the earth oxygen and carbon dioxide in equal measure.

"No," I say again, and Tom understands something, because he tells me just to drive to the end of the field, then, and I do. And when we get to the end of the field, Tom tells me to nose the little red truck over the hump of the road, and I do.

"Look both ways," he says, and I do. "Anything coming?"

Nothing coming. Tom tells me to drive the little red truck straight across the road, straight into the driveway, and flush with the porch, and I do. He tells me to push down on the clutch as I push down on the brake, and then to shift into first gear, and I do.

The engine ticks. The truck is motionless, solid and firm on the surface of the earth. But while we sit in the truck, parked on the packed earth driveway, tectonic plates are shifting beneath us. They are moving now, underneath the red Datsun, where Tom and I sit. Tom reaches across the stick shift and turns the ignition off, plucks out the key, and tosses it from hand to hand.

"Why did you do that with Jimmy Wilson?" Tom says.

Silence.

"Didn't you know he was nuts about you?"

Silence.

"He's been nuts about you his whole life."

Silence.

"Don't hurt someone who cares about you like that," Tom says. "You're not the only person in the world who's ever been hurt. Don't be cruel."

Cruel? The gorge comes over me again, rock below me, rock around me, and Jimmy Wilson with that look in his eyes. Tom inserts the key in the ignition again.

"Switch places with me," he says. "We're going up to Star Hill."

My mother gazes at us through the kitchen screen door. What is she thinking? What are her thoughts? Night after night she sits, her fingers moving. *Come with me, Mom.* One paper crane. *They don't know everything.* Two paper cranes. *Come with me.* Three paper cranes. *Don't hate me.*

"Okay, Rose," Tom says halfway up William T.'s hill. "Talk to me."

He looks over at me.

"You're supposed to keep your eyes on the road," I say. "Didn't you study that in your driver's manual? Didn't your grandfather teach you that when he took you out on the road for the first time?"

He will not be distracted.

"Talk to me."

"It's not Jimmy," I say. "It's me."

"Tell that to Jimmy."

"You don't get it."

"Try me. Maybe I get more than you think."

How to explain? What to explain? That I am still water that doesn't want to be still, that I want to be moving water, that the still water that is me wants out, wants to flow, wants to flow away, wants to change and pass through, be done?

Tom sits next to me, his hands and feet moving in harmony with the pedals and the wheel and the stick of his truck. Tom Miller of the stone in the village green, the gazebo, the drives in the darkness to lean against his father's name. Tom Miller of the haymow, and the rope swing, and the window in the barn that is less window and more door to the ether. Walk straight through it into sky. Sometimes at night now, I stand in the opening of that window-that-is-not-window and imagine falling.

What can I tell Tom? That I'm numb and I want to feel? That I thought Jimmy and the others would take the hurt from my heart and put it elsewhere, but I was wrong? It just stayed right there in my heart. *All Millers go through crazy,* William T. says. But I am Rose Latham, and I am going through crazy, and I can't find my way out of crazy.

"Out," I say. "I want out."

Ivy is joined to me through blood and bone and something else, something I can only sense. Her trappedness is my trappedness, and I am an animal caught in a trap who looks down and would chew her own leg off if she could, but I can't.

"I can't," I say. I shake my head. Nothing more to say.

We sit in Tom's truck on top of Star Hill. Star Hill is where the ghosts came out, where our friends come after parties and dances to park and wait for the ghosts and drink and make out. This is where Ivy and Joe used to come. I would lie awake until she came slipping back into the house, slipping up the stairs, slipping into the room, slipping out of her clothes, slipping between the sheets. I would lie awake until I heard her breathing slip into the slow soft breathing of a person who knew how to sleep. A person who knew how to be awake, and how to be asleep.

Hello, young doctor walking away down the hall. Helloooo, can you hear me? Do you ever think about my sister? Do you ever think about my mother, whirling in the hallway, her hands against her ears, her head shaking back and forth and back and forth? Can you still hear her voice?

"I cannot lose my daughter."

Do you ever think about what you said to her?

"Too late," you said. "Too late."

"Didn't you know Jimmy was nuts about you?" Tom says.

"I'm not nuts about Jimmy, though."

"I know you're not. That's what I'm talking about. Don't sleep with him if you don't care about him."

Sleep? I didn't sleep with Jimmy Wilson. We lay down together on the rocks at the gorge, rock beneath me, rock all around me, hard and unmoving. Far below us, tectonic plates grinding away.

"Don't break his heart on purpose."

"Don't break *his* heart?"

"Yeah. Don't."

"Whose heart is fucking breaking here?" I say.

His hand is loose on the stick shift, fingers relaxed.

"I don't know," he says. "You tell me."

Suddenly I hate him, hate Tom Miller, Tom Miller with his T-shirt fraying at the neck seam, his brown boots, his jeans with the hole in the knee. I hate Tom Miller, Tom Miller who drives at night to the stone in the village green, Tom Miller who regards me with his hazel eyes.

"Tell me," he says.

Still he gazes at me. Doesn't blink. My finger comes up and points at my own heart, my own pumping blindly away inside my chest.

"So you know what it feels like, then," he says. "Don't go breaking someone else's in the hope that you'll feel better. Because you won't."

His hand plays on the stick shift.

"But they all talk about her. They talk about her. They say she's a vegetable. As if she's not even there."

All around us evening is falling on the Sterns Valley. The view from Star Hill is the most beautiful view for miles and miles, and I can't see it. All I see is a girl in a hospital bed.

"Jimmy Wilson has nothing to do with what happened to Ivy," Tom says. "He hasn't done anything to you."

"Why don't you shut up about Jimmy Wilson?"

"Why don't you be angry if you're angry? Don't take it out on him."

"It's not just him," I say.

He looks at me. Those eyes.

"Warren," I say. "Todd."

Something flickers in his eyes. "Don't hurt yourself."

"I'll hurt myself if I want," I say, and even to my own ears I sound like a child.

"You're angry."

"I'm not angry. I'm sick of you, though. I can tell you that."

"You're angry."

"Who would I be angry at?"

"You tell me."

The sun is gone now. The Sterns Valley shimmers below us, bathed in the soft blues and grays and greens of a summer dusk. Ivy would have loved this.

"My mother."

"Why?"

"She hasn't once been to visit Ivy. She doesn't know what it's like. She makes William T. and me do it all. She sits there making those fucking cranes, and she doesn't even look at me. 'You never know,' she says. 'Miracles happen.' Miracles don't happen."

The lights in the Buchholzes' barn down below us in Sterns Corners glows brighter as dusk grows darker. William T. once told me that the Buchholzes dance naked in their barn at night.

"Maybe she needs to believe that miracles can happen," Tom says. "Maybe she's not like you—maybe she can't let Ivy go."

Let Ivy go?

Am I letting Ivy go?

"Hey," Tom says. "Hey."

But I can't stop crying. Water clogs my eyes and nose and throat, water flows out of me. Am I letting my sister go? Who am I, if not Ivy's sister? Who will I be, without her beside me?

Tears leak out of me everywhere, and there's nothing to blow my nose on but my sleeve, and then my sleeve is wet and filthy. Tom takes off his flannel shirt and drapes it over me. *Don't hurt someone who cares about you. Don't be cruel.*

"My heart is breaking," I tell him, and it's the truth. Your heart literally hurts when it's breaking. You can feel it, every beat another ache, and nothing you can do will stop it, either from beating or breaking.

CHAPTER TEN

"Why don't you drive us down today, Younger?" William T. says. "Now that you're getting the hang of it."

"What? Drive your truck?"

"That's the general idea."

"William T., the gas gauge doesn't even work. What if we run out of gas on Route 12?"

"If we run out of gas on Route 12, then we'll pull over. We'll *drift* over. In a gasless situation, *drift* is a better word."

"And you know all about gasless situations."

"Indeed I do," William T. agrees.

"Maybe we should ask my mother to come with us."

William T. is silent.

"You know, to break up the monotony of her life a little? Suggest to her that—surprise, surprise—the normal thing for a mother to do if her daughter's lying in a hospital bed is to go visit her."

Will the day come when my mother puts down her squares of paper, brushes aside her hundreds of origami cranes, and walks into Ivy's room? William T. pokes the butter knife into the place where, in a normal world, his key would go—he had to drill out his ignition a few weeks ago—and the engine starts up obediently.

"What kind of mother never once visits her daughter in the hospital?"

"The kind of mother who's doing what she can do."

"And what is that, exactly? A thousand paper cranes?"

"Yes."

"Give me a break."

"Why are you so angry, Younger?"

"Jesus," I say. "First Tom and now you. I'm angry at *her*."

"Who?"

"Her! My mother!"

"Are you sure it isn't Ivy?"

"No!"

But I'm crying again. Again I'm crying. William T.

pulls the truck over to the side of Glass Factory Road, about half a mile before the entrance to Route 12.

"Come here," he says, and he hauls me over the hump in the front seat until I'm sitting on his lap, a seventeen-year-old baby. He reaches over me and pounds on the broken glove compartment until it opens. A mound of fast-food napkins tumbles out. He wipes at my cheeks and eyes and rests his chin on top of my head as if I'm his baby daughter.

"How can you say I'm angry at Ivy?" I say.

"I didn't say you were. I only asked."

"But how can you even think that? It wasn't Ivy's fault."

"I know."

"My stupid mother should see her! Be with her! Visit her, her own daughter for God's sake!"

"Your mother's not normal."

I look at him. That is not something I ever expected to hear. He looks back at me steadily. Holds my gaze.

"You know it, Younger, and I know it. But she does the best she can."

I try to say, *Well, her best is not good enough,* but the words won't come out. Something in the world changed when William T. said what he said. *Your mother's not normal.* Something clicked into place. William T. is right, and his eyes are sad and tired.

"William T., were you mad at your son when he died?"

He doesn't flinch. "I was mad at the world," he says. "The entire world had let me down. Including him."

Together we sit in his truck, pulled over to the side of Glass Factory Road. Once in a while a car drones by. A bee flies in the open window, swoops around for a few seconds, hovers in the air before us, flies on out again.

"We all walk around with a stone in our shoe, Younger," William T. says. "You. Me. Crystal. Your mother. The whole entire world."

"Ivy left me," I say. "She left me behind."

"She did," William T. says. "She wouldn't have chosen to, but she did."

After a while I crawl back over the hump to the passenger side of the cab, and William T. sticks the butter knife back into the ignition. Onward.

Ivy and I had an accident. It was dusk in the Adirondacks, and the light blue truck came sliding and sliding. Can Ivy see her life at all anymore, somewhere way down deep inside her brain, her brain that's a line on a machine now? Can she remember that night in the haymow? All those nights in the haymow, all those nights when we were little, and then not so little, and we were growing up, and we were teenagers, and Joey turned into Joe and Rosie turned into Rose and Tommy turned into Tom, and Ivy stayed Ivy. Ivy began as Ivy and remains as Ivy.

Joe Miller turned to her that night and said, "What would you do if you weren't afraid, Ivy?"

And she jumped. A swoosh above our heads—we were all sitting on hay bales in the darkness—and she was up and away.

Through the paneless window she swung, and she disappeared, and there was no sound. She was gone. And we were up and running, out of the barn, down around the hill: "Ivy? Ivy! Ivy!" There she was, there on the rocks where she had fallen, the long flat rocks that surrounded the springhouse where the cool water comes bubbling out of the ground. The rocks that broke her arm and her ankle. We ran, and wove our arms together, and picked her up and carried her to the house, and into the car we went, and down to Utica, the hospital, the fluorescence, the white casts for the rest of the summer.

"Screw it," Ivy said. "It was worth it."

Joe didn't say he was sorry, sorry he goaded her, sorry he dared her. And she didn't ask him to.

My sister's heart is working, pumping and pumping and pumping. When that truck came sliding into us, were her hands on the steering wheel trying to steer away from the truck, steer anywhere, over a guardrail into a tree, anywhere to get away from the truck that wouldn't stop coming? Were her hands on the windshield, trying to push the truck away from her?

I don't know. My own eyes were closed.

The only thing I know for sure was that in the end, her arm came out and smashed against my chest. Like mothers do with their babies. My sister was trying to keep me safe.

"Did you?" she said to me in the lucid interval, that brief span of time before the hemorrhage spread too far and shut her down. "Did you?"

Did I what, Ivy? Sister, tell me.

I'm in the green chair with my Pompeii book. William T. is behind me, reading about the bird of the day, which is the hermit thrush, the only brown thrush likely in cold weather. When the hermit thrush is alarmed, it flicks its wings and raises and lowers its tail. Its call note? A nasal *vreeeee.*

"Imagine it," I pretend-read. "All those ordinary people, living their ordinary lives. Maybe the baby had just gone to sleep in his basket of rushes in the corner."

"Jesus," William T. says. "We're back to Moses again?"

"The baby is asleep in his basket of rushes, and his mother stands at the clay oven baking the bread for lunch," I pretend-read. "His father is at the marketplace selling homemade wine."

Angel peeks in and sees that all is well—Rose in the green chair with the book, William T. in the blue chair with his hermit thrush—and waves from the door as she lets it close again.

"And then, perhaps, there came the sound," I pretend-read. "There might well have been a sound. Would it have been the sound of ash filling the air? Did it make a sound like the beating of wings?"

The sounds I most love: hail, rattling on the deck or pounding the hood of the truck; snow, the softness of it when I wake up on a winter night and feel the world around me muffled; rain, in spring or summer when it drums on the roof and lulls me into sleep; crickets chirping or bullfrogs down at the pond, croaking their way through a soft summer night.

And my sister's voice. *It's happening again, isn't it, Rosie? Come on—let's walk.*

Volcanic ash. Would it have a sound?

"You look up from checking the bread, which is almost finished baking," I pretend-read. "You know that something is wrong. Your first instinct is to look in the corner and make sure the baby is all right. The baby is all right. The baby is sleeping. But still, something is wrong. You can sense it."

"That Pompeii book is strange," William T. says. "It's not written like a typical history book."

Was the baby in the rush basket scooped up by his mother when the ash first began to flutter down? Did his mother tilt her head and listen to a faraway sound that she didn't understand? Did the baby wake? Did he begin to cry? Did his mother try to soothe him as she hurried from the house?

Or maybe there was no time. Maybe it all happened so fast that there was only a single moment of confusion—she looked at the oven where the bread was baking; she looked at the bed, which was still unmade; she found herself running to the corner where the baby lay sleeping in his rush basket—and then it was all over.

Ivy has the hair she's always wanted now. Long and soft, softer than she could have imagined.

"It's finer than baby hair," Angel said. "It's a marvel of hair. Look at it."

She held up a strand. Light from the window behind her poured in and illuminated my sister's hair. Who would have known that each individual strand could contain within it so many colors, could glisten in the rays of the sun as if it were made of the sun itself?

"'Before going on to Chapter Six,'" I say, "'make sure you can answer these questions. What is the hand signal for a stop? A right turn? If two drivers enter an intersection from opposite directions at the same time, one going straight, the other turning left, which must yield the right of way? If you enter an intersection to make a left turn but oncoming traffic prevents you from making the turn right away, what should you do? If you reach an uncontrolled intersection at the same time as a driver on your right and both of you are going to go straight, who has the right of way? What must you do if you are entering a road from a driveway? You are facing a green light, but traffic on the other side of the intersection would keep you from going all the way through the intersection. May you enter the intersection? Does a vehicle about to enter a traffic circle or rotary have the right of way over vehicles already in the circle?'"

"Jesus H. Christ," William T. says. "The hell if I know the answer to half those questions."

"See?" I say. "That's what I've been telling you. It's not that easy."

Then I hear the sound of my mother's voice.

"Ivy?"

She carries a big cardboard box. Her cranes, her hundreds and hundreds of cranes. There she stands, at the foot of Ivy's bed. The ventilator: *wishhh, wishhh, wishhh.*

"Connie," William T. says. "Connie."

She looks over at him. There's a look in her eyes. The box of cranes looks so heavy, cradled in her arms like that. She looks at William T. and her head begins to shake. *No,* her head says. *No.*

"Connie."

William T. gets up from the blue chair. He takes the

big box of cranes from my mother and sets it on the floor. Then he picks up the hairbrush from the nightstand, Ivy's hairbrush, and puts it into my mother's hand. He folds her hand around it, as if she's a toddler and he is her parent, trying to show her how to hold a spoon.

"Here you go," he says. "Sit down now. Younger, give your mother a seat, will you?"

I stand up and William T. guides my mother into the green chair.

"There you go," he says. "Brush now. Brush her hair."

He puts his hand over my mother's hand and guides her hand to Ivy's head, and down he brushes, down they brush, down the brush glides over my sister's hair. My mother's other hand comes hesitating up and follows the path of the brush. After a while Angel is there, turning Ivy's chart around and around in her hands.

"Angel," William T. says, "I'd like you to meet Connie."

"Nice to meet you, Connie."

"She's the mother. Elder and Younger's mother."

"Of course she is," Angel agrees.

We all stand there, watching my mother brush Ivy's hair. One hand strokes the brush through Ivy's hair, and the other hand follows in the path of the brush, smoothing and smoothing. It's a rhythm, and my mother falls into it. Strands fly up in the air to meet the brush.

The night of the accident, my mother stood in the hallway with the doctors and the nurses around her. She was the lone tree in the middle of supplicant trees. Her hands covered her ears. Her eyes were closed. "I cannot lose my daughter," she said. She kept on saying it. "I cannot lose my daughter."

"Too late," the young doctor said. "Your daughter is already dead. In every meaningful way, your daughter is already gone."

"You don't know," my mother said. "You don't know! You have no fucking idea of what my daughter will or will not be able to do!"

The young doctor shook his head. He was angry; he was impatient with my mother. *Crazy woman,* he was thinking—I could tell.

"You! Don't! Know!" my mother said. She started pushing at him, at his white coat, his chest. "You have No! Fucking! Idea!"

And the doctor turned and walked away down the hall and disappeared.

Later, William T. held my mother against his truck. He and Crystal and Spooner and Tom had brought us home from the hospital. Tom and I stood on the porch, and the three of them stood around my mother there in the chill March air, closed ranks around her, and William T.'s arms circled themselves around my mother and she leaned into his arms, and her head was on his shoulder, and his arms were wrapped around her. Tom and I watched from the porch. My mother leaned against William T., and William T.'s arms were wrapped around her, and William T. and Crystal leaned against each other, and of the three of them, none either moved or spoke until my mother's shoulders started to shake and I knew she was crying.

"It's okay," William T. whispered to her. "It's okay."

My mother's shoulders aren't narrow, but her rib cage is the narrowest of rib cages. Turn her sideways and there is not much there. Ivy too. When they stood together, their bodies were the same, Ivy's smaller, but the bones were put together in precisely the same way. When Ivy walked, I could feel my mother walking.

William T.'s hands came up and touched my mother's hair. She didn't move.

The hand that was touching my mother's hair began to stroke her hair. Down it went, from the crown of her head to where her hair brushed against her shoulders. And up again, and down. Smoothing, and stroking, and smoothing, and stroking. Never changing its rhythm. William T.'s eyes gazed at Crystal, who was crying silently, and his hand moved as if it were its own self, as if it knew what to do independent of any thought, as if it were stroking my mother's hair out of instinct alone: *Yes. This is what must be done.*

My mother couldn't lose her daughter. She couldn't

say the words that would let them disconnect the ventilator from Ivy's body, let Ivy's body gradually cease to take in air, let her heart gradually stop its squeezing, its squeezing, its squeezing.

"So she's not brain-dead?" she said.

The young doctor looked away.

"She tried to take a breath, so that means she's not brain-dead, right?"

He looked away, kept looking away, shook his head.

"Not officially," is what he finally said. "Not legally."

My mother keeps brushing Ivy's hair, and then she puts the brush down. She pulls Ivy's hair to one side and plaits it. Unplaits it. Strokes her fingers through its long softness. Finger-combs it. Bends her cheek to the long strands and breathes in. Breathes out. She turns to me and William T.

"I wish I had let her go right in the beginning," she whispers. "I wish that I had let her go."

CHAPTER ELEVEN

The day comes when I am sitting in the green chair by my sister's bed. No more Pompeii. No more baby in his rush basket, baby who will never wake up. Goodbye, baby. Goodbye, mother who couldn't save him.

I read from the driver's manual. Getting ready for my road test, three days hence.

"It's time, Younger," William T. says. "You can't just sit in that goddamned chair reading from that manual forever."

"That's a quarter."

He ignores me. Maybe he thinks I'm old enough now

that curses will not adversely affect my growth. Maybe he figures I'm tall enough now to be safe.

"There comes a time, Younger," he says, "when the book must be put aside, and the pedal put to the metal. And that time, by God, has come."

He turns in his blue chair and points his index finger out the window, at the gray thread of pavement winding its way beyond the Rosewood Convalescent Home driveway.

"Road ho!" he says, and turns to Ivy in her bed. "What do you think, Elder? Is it time that Younger got off her butt and into the driver's seat?"

Ivy says nothing. *Wishhh, wishhh, wishhh.* My sister, beautiful sister with the softest hair in the world, sister whose hair was never so soft when she was alive.

And what I never wanted to happen has just happened. I thought the words *when she was alive.*

I didn't mean it, Ivy! Ivy, I didn't mean it! Ivy, I am not letting you go!

She doesn't open her eyes and look at me and say, *I know you didn't mean it.*

She doesn't say, *But, Rosie, what you said is true. I used to be alive, but I'm not anymore.*

She doesn't say, *Please, Rosie, let me go.*

It's me who is alive. I can walk through that door over there. I can shove it open with both hands and stride down that hall. I can turn the corner and disappear. I can walk all the way back up to the Adirondacks if I want to, because I am alive. I am *alive,* and my body pumps itself full of oxygen and my blood runs free and I'm alive, alive, alive.

A bird alights on the windowsill and looks around, looks into the room where I sit in the green chair and William T. sits in the blue chair and Ivy lies in the bed with her hands folded. The bird sees that our room is a small place with high walls. No way to see the wide world from in there, the world that the bird has hovered in all its life. And with one beat of its wings, the bird is up and out, spreading its wings to the world. Goodbye, sad windowsill to a sad room.

My heart that's been cracking and cracking and cracking cracks open. Pieces lie in shards around me, tiny pieces of the blue sky shattered and fallen to earth. I stand up.

"Let's go," I say to William T.

And William T., surprised but silent, stands up too.

Tom Miller comes to my house late that evening, walks into the kitchen when I don't answer the door, walks through the living room and finds my mother, working on her thousand paper cranes. He tells me later that he followed her finger, pointing silently to the haymow where I am hiding, a refugee from the water that is again flooding its banks, threatening to drown me.

Silence. With my eyes closed, the world swirls around me and dizziness comes creeping. Am I standing? Lying down? Where is the paneless window? The dark air of the haymow, still and heavy, presses against me and it's hard to breathe. Breathe. Breathe. Breathe. I open my eyes. Tom stands before me.

I reach my hand out to him.

"Tom."

We stand in the darkness of the haymow, and he wraps his arms around me. I pull my arms out from under his and put them around his neck. I bury my face in his shoulder. He smells of sun, and of hay, and of sweat and soap. He smells of himself. We stand and rock back and forth, a tiny movement, a pendulum made of the two of us. Back. And forth. And back. And forth.

"Come here," he says.

He whispers, "Come here."

He lays me down in the hay. Our arms wrap around each other. He kisses the top of my head.

"Don't hurt yourself any more," he says.

I close my eyes and picture myself at the gorge. A bird's-eye view, as if I'm a bird hovering over my own self, my own self with Jimmy, with Warren, with Todd. If I move they might think I like it. They might think I'm with them, part of what's happening, instead of hovering above, watching and hoping: Is this a way to get away? To be moving water instead of trapped within myself and overflowing? I don't move. Beside me the water of the gorge tumbles in its rushing way, scurrying over the rocks, on the way to its temporary resting place, Hinckley Reservoir.

"Do you walk around with a stone in your shoe?" I whisper to Tom. "A stone that's your father?"

He laughs. "That's one way to look at it," he says.

Does the water of the Sterns Gorge know where it's going? Does it know that soon it will stop rushing, soon it will stop moving, soon it will be part of an immense body of still water? Viewed from space, the ocean appears as a giant body of still water. There is no way out.

"This hurts so much."

Tom tightens his arms.

"I want it to go away," I say.

"I know you do."

I close my eyes again, there in the haymow. It's a summer night in the Adirondacks, and the hay is new and the scent of cut grass, which is what hay is, rises around us. The hay is new and not as scratchy as it will be later. It still holds the scent of life lived outdoors, life lived in the sun and the rain and the wind. I love the smell of hay. We rock together in the haymow, Tom and I. I feel him against me. How different this is, from the boys at the gorge. A fluttering begins in my stomach and creeps through my body, down to my center, where I hollow out, and feel myself warm and soften.

"Tom?"

He shakes his head, there in the darkness.

"No," he says. I lay there, wrapped in his arms, and listen to his words echo in my mind.

"No?"

"That's right," he says. "We're just going to lie here."

I ease onto my back and look up into the cavernous space of the barn above us. Somewhere above the peaked tin roof, bats wheel and swoop in the darkness. A barred owl calls from the woods down the dirt road. I listen for an answer, and in a minute it comes, from the pine woods across the road. *Who, who, who are you? Who, who, who are you?*

Tom turns on his side and rocks me in his arms. We don't kiss. At some point in the night, the owls cease to call and the whippoorwill halts his lament. The paneless window appears as a blur of lighter darkness that turns into a rectangle of indigo, turns into the blue of my mother's winter sweater, turns into aqua, turns into the pink-white of a dawn sky.

Tom sleeps. He lies on his stomach with his arms pillowing his head. I prop myself on my arm and look at him. He sleeps, not moving.

I watch his back through the T-shirt to see how he

breathes in his sleep. No motion. No motion. No motion. Is he alive?—and then, motion. The slight lift of worn cotton, and then the slight drift downward. No motion. No motion. No motion. Then: the slight lift. The slight drift.

Breathe in the smell of his hair. It curves over his head, following the shape of his skull. Maybe he cuts it himself. It's the kind of haircut that needs no instructions to the barber.

"Just do something different," I've heard women say at the hairdresser's. "I'm so damned sick of the way I look."

Not Tom Miller. I watch him sleeping. His T-shirt, his jeans, his running shoes that sometime in the middle of the night he must have taken off because they lie next to us. His hair. The no-motion, no-motion, no-motion, slight-lift, slight-drift, of his back. His lungs inside, doing their work. His heart, pumping, pumping, pumping. His blood, flowing its way through all the passages and curves of his body. Is he dreaming?

I shiver and Tom wakes. It's light enough to see his eyes open.

"Are you cold?" he says. "Baby, are you cold?"

He turns so that his arms are around me again.

Baby, are you cold?—and the ball of hurt inside me swells. How much it hurts. Every day it hurts all over again, waking up in that dreamy half-moment when you have no strength in your body and you're still limp from a night of sleep. In that half-moment, my long strong fingers—fingers that can pull up any weed, that can push and pull at dough, fingers that can shuck an ear of sweet corn in three firm tugs—can't clench. Helpless. Baby fingers.

Every morning it comes over me again, that Ivy's not in our house. It comes to me in a wave, another wave, another wave, engulfing me. Every morning I lie in bed until my muscles can move. And then I get up. And go into the kitchen. Bare feet. Splintery floor. And I make the coffee. And when the coffee is made, I stand at the bottom of the stairs and call up:

"Coffee, Mom!"

Every morning I say it in the same tone of voice. I tried to make it a routine, right after the accident. *See,* I was trying to say to my mother, back in March. *See? This is a life that still has coffee in it, coffee in the morning.* Every morning I open the cupboard and take out her favorite mug, the one with the daffodils on it, and set it on the counter next to the pot of coffee. Take the half-and-half out of the refrigerator. Pour it into the daffodil mug. Measure in the sugar.

"Coffee, Mom!"

And down she comes.

"Thanks, Rose."

That's it. That's our morning routine now. *Coffee, Mom. Thanks, Rose.*

Coffeemomthanksrose, Coffeemomthanksrose, Coffeemomthanksrose, Coffeemomthanksrose, Coffeemomthanksrose. Soon it will be time to go into the house and make the coffee, so that the routine can be followed. But why follow the routine? What's the point? I bury my head in Tom's shoulder, and his hand strokes down my hair, down and down, and I feel his lips on the top of my head. He kisses the top of my head and says nothing. My hair is electric, softened, calmed, all at once, by the stroking of Tom's hand. All the mornings since March are running through me—*Coffeemomthanksrose*—flooding over me, and there in the haymow I know how much they have cost me.

"Every morning I make her coffee," I whisper into Tom's shoulder. "Every morning I get down her mug."

I shake my head against his shoulder. He pulls my head up and puts both hands on the sides of my face.

"Hey," he says. He whispers it against my ear. I breathe him in, his Tom Miller smell of warm skin and sun and soap and sweat. He smells like himself. He smells like life.

"They're never going to look at her and know who she was," I say. "They're never going to know who Ivy was."

He doesn't ask who *they* are, all the *theys* out there, all the people who will ever push their way through the door of the room where Ivy sleeps and walk up to her bed, pick up the chart that hangs for all eternity at the foot of the bed, and study it. *Look at her,* I want to scream to all the imaginary people pushing their way through that door—*Look at her! Can't you even say hello to her before you pick up that chart, that goddamned chart?*

Quarter, please. Another quarter. Clink. The flowered ceramic jar is filling up. Almost time to take it to the bank, turn it into real money.

What else would I give up?

What would they want, what would appease them, those who want me to give things up so that my sister can come back?

Would I give up my father, down there in his park in New Orleans, the jazz band playing softly around him, tourists with their hot beignets strolling past where he lies sleeping? My father, who I used to pray to God to love me. *Please, God, make my father love me.*

Yes. I would give up my father.

Take it all, you gods. Take whatever you want, you who have it within your power to bring my sister back and yet aren't doing it.

Years of your life. We want years of your life.

Okay. Take some, then.

As many as we want.

Go ahead. Take whatever the hell you want. Just bring my sister back to me.

How many years of life do I have left?

I see myself as an old, old lady. Sitting in a rocking chair covered with sweaters and blankets. My hair is gray—no, my hair is not gray because I'm hairless. I gave up my hair to try to get my sister back, back when I was a child. Remember? I'm drinking sugarless tea that someone else made for me because I'm too weak and old to move from my rocking chair. Every night someone carries me to bed and tucks me in with an electric blanket, because I'm always cold the way all old ladies are always cold. Poor circulation.

How many years do I have left?

Six.

Take them. You can have them. All six of them.

No. Those aren't the years we want. We want some of the other years. The years in which you can move, years when you are not wearing nine sweaters one on top of the other, years when everyone you love is still alive and you can still climb a mountain in the Adirondacks and sit on top and look out at those fall colors, flame on flame on flame. Those, those are the years we want.

If there is nothing I will not give up to bring back my sister, does that mean my own life? Would I give up my own life?

There comes a point at which you stop giving things up. That is what I won't give up. None of it will I give up, for my beautiful sister Ivy who lies in the bed. Ivy who used to be alive. Ivy who used to be. Ivy who used. Ivy who.

Ivy-who-is-not-me.

Not me. Not me. Not me.

CHAPTER TWELVE

"What about the Miller boy?"

"Tom Miller? What about him?"

My mother gazes at me. Her fingers are busy with her cranes. She left the big box of them down in Ivy's room, but the big box wasn't enough, she said. "There's only eight hundred there," she said. "I need one thousand." She can do them without looking now. She makes them out of anything. Newspaper. The Sunday comics. Cartoon faces of people with big noses, cats and small birds and dogs with enormous sad eyes peek from the graceful finished cranes, the nearly thousand cranes made by my mother.

"Do you love him?"

"Yes."

She nods. Once. A brief, businesslike nod.

"He's a good boy."

So much is left out of *Do you love him?* and *Yes.* So much is left out, such as what it felt like that night in the haymow. I want to tell someone about Tom Miller, and how his arms felt around me, and how I remember him sitting at his desk by the window last fall, the way all the colors of the world were caught and held in the leaves that spun and floated down to the earth. About the night we sat at his father's stone in the village green, that night when the air was soft and the crickets were chirping and the moon hung round and full, so many million miles away. I wanted to tell Tom about Pompeii, about the baby in its rush basket in the corner, the baby who never knew what was coming. How when the ash came to cover the town, it did not spin and drift gently from a blue, blue sky. Ash came in a fury, a fury of black and gray that blotted out all sound, all air, all life.

My mother works on her paper cranes. No more questions about Tom Miller. She doesn't know how he circled his arms around my ribs.

"Feel how tight my arms are around you?" he said. "This is how tight I'll be holding you. No matter where you go, or where I go, remember how tight I'm holding you."

Memory doesn't fade. You don't forget. When you

conjure something that happened, float it back up through time and space, it will happen again. When I am eighty years old and looking back on my life, I will be back in the haymow with Tom Miller, that night when he held me so tight.

Cranes hang now from the ceiling of Ivy's room. One after another my mother kept on making them. She sat in the blue chair while William T. sat in an orange chair on wheels that Angel the nurse moved in for him. She took all kinds of paper: newspaper, pages from a magazine, Christmas wrappings, a page from the Utica phone book. She turned the paper into a square by folding it against itself and then folding and ripping off the excess. She paid no attention to dimension. The cranes were of all shapes and sizes.

"Do you ever measure, Connie?" Angel asked. They were on a first-name basis. Connie and Angel.

"No, Angel, I don't."

Now Angel looks up at the cranes dangling from the ceiling. My mother strings them on thread and separates each with a piece of straw cut from the drinking straws you get at fast-food places. Sometimes, when I'm in the truck with her on the way to visit Ivy, I drive through a drive-thru.

"Order?"

"Three straws."

"Excuse me?" the microphone voice squawks.

"Three straws."

Pause.

"And what else?"

"Nothing."

Pause.

"Drive up to window number one."

We drive up to window number one. "Three straws." "Thank you." "You're welcome, come again."

My road test has come and gone. When the day came, William T. and Tom drove me down to it in the Datsun, so that I could take the test in the rusting red Datsun, the truck I learned to drive in, the truck with the stick shift that, according to William T., is like butter. "Damn, those Japanese know how to make a shift," William T. said. "Beats Detroit all hollow."

The man who gave me the road test had a clipboard like the clipboard that hung at the end of Ivy's bed. I was calm throughout my test, and so was he. When it came time to parallel park, I did so perfectly. I followed the man's instructions through downtown Utica, and every five seconds I glanced in my rearview mirror. I braked. I pressed the gas appropriately. I made sure my seat belt was buckled securely.

"Well?" I said at the end, when the man told me to pull over to the curb.

You're not supposed to ask anything about your

performance on the road test. You're not supposed to ask if you passed or if you failed, but I asked anyway. What the hell, as William T. would have said.

"Well, what?" the man said. He didn't smile.

"Did I pass?"

He regarded me. He gave me an appraising look, and I looked right back at him. Maybe he could tell I was older than my years. Maybe he could tell that I am a seventeen-year-old girl who has been through war, and that I don't have a lot of time for nonsense.

"All I can tell you, Miss Latham," he said, "is that I will never see you again."

Good enough.

The first night I had my license, I got in the Datsun and drove up to Jimmy Wilson's house. *Knock. Knock.* Jimmy came to the door and froze when he saw it was me. I knew he didn't want to talk to me, but he was too polite just to slam it and walk away.

"I just wanted to tell you I'm sorry," I said.

He looked at me.

"I wanted something that would take it away," I said. "Make me forget."

He kept looking at me.

"It didn't have anything to do with you," I said. "I wanted to feel something, I guess. I know that sounds weird. I was hurting so much."

He looked at me for a long time.

"I would never want to hurt you, Rose," he said. "Ever."

There was a lump in my throat, at the sound of his voice, so quiet and hesitant. I nodded. *I didn't want to hurt you, either, Jimmy, but I did.* Turned around and got back into the Datsun.

Cranes hang from the window frames of Ivy's room, from the light switch, the lamps, the bed rail, the overhead light. Cranes hang from strings attached to unbent paper clips, threaded through cup hooks screwed into the ceiling. William T.'s work, all of it.

"Be careful," I said when he stood on his blue chair.

"Mmm."

When they were all hooked, he dusted off his hands. A job well done. Origami cranes sway slightly, fluttering in the air of the room. The closest we come to cranes in the Adirondacks are herons. I saw a great blue heron once. It stood by the shore of Deeper Lake, one leg up, one leg down. It bent and dipped its long beak toward the cool dark water.

My mother, my not-normal mother, made the cranes for her daughter. *Don't underestimate your mother,* William T. says. *She does the best she can.* A thousand cranes hang above Ivy, trembling in the air that displaces itself whenever the door to her room opens and someone slips in. My mother, me, William T., Angel, or the doctor.

We all slip in.

We slip in because we don't want Ivy to be startled,

there on her bed, where she lies in her long silent prayer. We don't want any more crashing, startling, loud noises that end in pain. Hasn't Ivy had enough of that? Haven't we all?

William T. held my mother against his truck, the day of the accident, and stroked her hair while his girlfriend, Crystal, stood next to them and wept.

Tom Miller drives in the dark to the stone that bears his father's name.

Spooner sits in the sun and canes.

My mother spends her days righting tipped bottles and her nights working on her cranes. I watched her the other day rip a sheet of paper from Ivy's clipboard and make a crane out of it, out of that torn written-on chart.

And what do I do? How do I get away from that light blue truck, sliding and sliding—it will slide forever—into and onto and through my beautiful Ivy, whose arm was flung out against my chest to protect me?

We all walk around with a stone in our shoe.

"So, the Miller boy," my mother says. "Do you love him?"

"Yes."

My mother regards me from the rocking chair. I feel the full force of her gaze. I say nothing. She regards me awhile longer, and I say nothing for that while.

You are most powerful when you are most silent. People never expect silence. They expect words, motion, defense, offense, back and forth. They expect to leap into the fray. They are ready, fists up, words leaping forth from their mouths. Silence? No.

My mother knows the power of silence too. She rarely uses it, but she has the power. She uses her power now. She stills her body. She almost never stills her body, and it takes her some time. First, she stops the motion of the rocking chair. Then she draws her legs up and crosses them on the chair. Then she places each hand on one knee and spreads her fingers so not one touches another. Then she closes her eyes. She calms her breathing. She becomes as motionless as is possible for my mother to become. She draws herself inward.

"Sometimes we go to the haymow," I say, when enough time has gone by so that she knows I can be as silent as her.

She doesn't move.

"And sometimes we go down to the village green," I say. "His father's stone is there. He likes to sit by it at night."

And that's all I say. Then I wait. My turn.

"I remember Chase Miller," my mother says after a long time of waiting. "He went to the war when I was a little girl." And after a longer time, my mother says, "Are you safe?"

"No."

It's the only thing to say. Are any of us safe? How do

we make it through? How, when you know you are going to leave this life whether you want to or not—when you know that you and everyone you love will leave this life—do we make it? I don't want to die. I don't want to die. *I don't want to die.*

My mother sits silently in her rocking chair. I go out on the porch and watch the sky turn plum like a days-old bruise. Tilt my head back and gaze up to where the pale moon hangs silent, a curved white hook. It's only August but already I can feel the longing of winter for itself, how the air and ground wait for ice, the snow that falls so deep in upstate New York and turns all living things to stone.

I sit on the porch steps and watch as bats pour out of the hole in the upper screened window of the old barn. They swoop and twirl and head off, singly and in small groups, diving and wheeling for bugs in the gathering dusk. When it's fully dark, I slip off the steps and into the night.

Some nights it's William T.'s corn field across the road, with its stalks feet taller than I am tall, silky brown tassels at the top of each ear. Cow corn, big-kerneled, hard and dry. I feel my way toes first, arms out to keep my balance.

Tonight it's the pine woods down from the corn field. Everyone is sleeping: my mother in her dreamless sleep, Ivy in Utica in whatever sleep comes to her now. I sit and draw my knees up and circle them with my arms, fold myself into the shape of an egg. I still my body to the stillness of the trees.

Owls call.

Small animals nose their way through the pines.

Bats flap and swoop overhead.

After a while my breathing slows and my skin becomes the same temperature as the summer night air. I sit patiently and wait. For what, I don't know.

Sometimes I walk the three miles that connect Route 274 with Sterns Valley Road with the packed dirt of Williams Road. Sometimes Tom comes with me. Sometimes I'm by myself. I walk through waves of warm air and waves of cold, their variation caused by something I don't understand, something that, had I asked Mr. Carmichael back in science, he would have been able to explain to me.

The starry night holds things I can't yet see: trees waiting for light, lakes ringed by pines, birds that sing only in the absence of sun. I'm used to the darkness, used to biding my time. A whippoorwill calls, keening in the distance once, twice, three times. On the other side of me, another returns the call.

Or is it an echo? Back and forth comes the call, birds mourning in their harsh language. That first night we were together, in the haymow, Tom Miller and I whispered back and forth, our mouths so close that I could feel the faint intake of his breath. I breathed in rhythm with him. His hand was light on my head, stroking my hair back, and back, and back.

The slender moon floats above the white pines like a buoy in the darkness. I lie on my back in the dew-wet grass and look up at the stars, glittering. One blinks out as I gaze at it. If it doesn't reappear, have I been witness to its death?

Ivy didn't care about the stars.

"Planet Earth is my sole terrain," she said.

"What about all the other worlds out there?" I said. "Pompeii. Hinckley Reservoir. String theory and the Higgs boson and all those millions and millions of stars?"

"Nope."

"Why?"

"Because."

"Because why?"

"For God's sake, Rosie. I'm not like you. This one world right here is enough for me."

Ivy is going now. She will be gone soon. Ivy and I had an accident. It was dusk in the Adirondacks that night, and a light blue truck came sliding around the curve, and now time is turning for my Ivy, curving upon its own axis, plucking her up and setting her down somewhere else, a somewhere I can't imagine.

I read to her for the last time today from the manual, and then I closed it. I'm a driver now. No more need to study up on the rules of the road. I put my hands over my sister's.

"William T.," I said. "Are there things worse than dying?"

William T. was sitting in the blue chair. He had completed his entire book of birds. "Just when you think you're done," he had said, "along come a thousand new cranes of indeterminate breed." His hands were quiet in his lap, and he stared up at the paper cranes fluttering in the breeze from the window, the paper cranes dancing above my sister.

"Living without love is worse than dying, Younger."

"But would you give up love if you could have your son back?"

"Not possible," he said. "My son was my love."

Love is my mother, her restless hands turning paper into birds. Love is William T., standing at his stove stirring me eggs soft and slow with plenty of butter. Love is Ivy, silhouetted for one moment in the dark outline of the paneless window. Still water, flow within me, flow through me; no one can love my world as I do.

"Yes," my mother said. "Let her go."

And they nodded. Cranes fluttered around us like ribbons, like streams, like white balloons drifting skyward, and William T.'s hands came out and covered my mother's hands.

There was a dark night when I sat in a circle in the haymow. Forbidden cigarettes, forbidden beer, forbidden time, and we were so alive, and our world was limitless.

"What would you do if you weren't afraid?" Joe Miller said to my sister.

And she jumped to her feet. It was night. The moon hung high in the night sky, drowning out the stars. I couldn't see her eyes. Her eyes had disappeared into the blackness that was night. The soft crush of bare feet on baled hay came to my ears and my sister was running; I knew only that she was running.

There in the darkness, Ivy found her way to the top of the teetering stack of hay bales. Joe Miller stood in the darkness and circled his arms around himself, circled them in the air, ranging farther and farther from the circle where we all sat, until his fingers found the thick twine of the rope swing. A single bat of his arm sent it in the direction of the invisible Ivy.

"Got it!"

For the rest of my life, I will hear that moment in my mind. "Got it!" she called, full of momentary delight. Joe Miller sat down—I could tell by the displacement of air—and we waited.

And then there was a swoosh, and my sister was passing above us all, whooping in triumph. Everything that came later would come, but first, there was that moment, that moment of Ivy above us, whirling above us through the darkness, out the paneless window toward the moon, toward the unfathomable reaches of space, and laughing.

ACKNOWLEDGMENTS

Thanks to Julie and Kate, unshakable compadres and first readers. Thanks to Kara LaReau for her astute and insightful editing. Thanks to Mark Engelstad for his articulate explanation of the physiology of brain trauma. Finally, thanks to my Steuben touchstones: the Ankens and the Bretts and, most especially, my parents.